GRQ

(GET RICH QUICK)

STEVEN BERNSTEIN

First published 3rd June 2025 by Fly on the Wall Press
Published in the UK by
Fly on the Wall Press
56 High Lea Rd
New Mills
Derbyshire
SK22 3DP

www.flyonthewallpress.co.uk
ISBN: 9781915789464
EBook: 9781915789471
Copyright Steven Bernstein © 2025

The right of Steven Bernstein to be identified as the author of this work has been asserted in accordance with the Copyright, Designs and Patents Act 1988. Cover design and typesetting by Isabelle Kenyon.

All rights reserved. No part of this publication may be reproduced, stored in or introduced into a retrieval system, or transmitted in any form, or by any means (electronic, mechanical, photocopying, recording or otherwise) without prior written permissions of the publisher. Any person who does any unauthorised act in relation to this publication may be liable for criminal prosecution and civil claims for damages.

A CIP Catalogue record for this book is available from the British Library.

EU GPSR Authorised Representative
LOGOS EUROPE, 9 rue Nicolas Poussin, 17000, LA ROCHELLE, France
E-mail: Contact@logoseurope.eu

I am grateful for my undoing and to those who undid me.
Now to start again.
At the beginning.

T.W. Suicide, grief

1. DO YOU WANT TO BE RICH? ASK ME HOW

GRQ. The miracle you can buy. That's what this story is about. It's not my story, but I'm an essential part. You might think, *he would say that, wouldn't he*? But, as it turns out, I really am an important part of this story. Because I am a maker of dreams.

You should give me a call if you want to get rich. Maybe you don't. But if you do, we can talk later.

And Marlon. Marlon, I changed his life. But is he grateful? Don't count on loyalty when you're dealing with finance, or I guess love or friendship. Or business. Just as a general principle, don't count on loyalty at all.

If you want a friend, get a dog. I say this all the time. If you want a friend, get a dog. And then pause for effect. It doesn't always get the laugh I want.

Marlon, he who should have been grateful, at the least, Marlon, that *fuckity, fuck, fuck* as I sometimes called him afterward, had a huge problem. Back then. When he wasn't grateful. He was lying to his wife. All the time. *Okay*, you will say, *so what*? But this wasn't your normal level of lying – these were big lies. *Whoppers*, my aunt called them. (She also used to call me her *little cattle rustler*. Kind of a Western thing. It doesn't matter. She isn't in the story. She died tragically in a farming accident, which made the whole *little cattle rustler thing* more poignant, as she would have said. She liked words like *poignant* and would use them around me as an example of how I might speak if I became a person who used words like *poignant*. I don't generally. But sometimes I try as kind of an homage to her.)

By the way, that isn't actually how she died.

2. FUTURE FAKING

Do you know the term future-faking? I hadn't heard it either until I met Marlon. I like the term. Now I use it, so people know I am up to date. If you aren't up to date, it means promising something in the future to get something now. Because of the 'faking' part, it sounds bad. *I will love you forever*, that sort of thing.

Also used in religions. Heaven and so on. (I have a lot of clients who are making money in the religion-space, so I mean no offense.) Cults. Health foods. Anything that relies on either hope or faith to generate income. Or just good feeling. A person on the deck of a sinking ship telling you, you are probably getting rescued. You probably aren't. None of us are.

3. THE RELIABLE NARRATOR

In literature, my aunt used to tell me (she read a lot, smoked smelly French cigarettes called Gauloises and never married), there is someone called the *unreliable narrator*. They tell you a story, but you realize after a while, they are BS-ing you, so you don't know what's true and what isn't because they are being their *unreliable selves*.

But I am a reliable self. Person. Whatever. My point is this: I am someone you should trust. Here is a good lesson I learned from experience. Usually, you shouldn't trust a person who asks you to trust them. I mean, if they are telling you the truth, why are they worried you won't believe them? But I am the exception. Also, it will be tough to tell you this story if you think I am an unreliable narrator. Because then, with everything I say, you will think: *he is BS-ing me*. And then what? You see what I mean? The world is built on trust. So sometimes it is best just to say to hell with it; *I will trust this guy*.

By the way, that's usually one of the first things I say on the phone when proposing a crypto-currency investment. I say, *Hi. I am really pleased to give you a unique opportunity, and no matter what you have heard about crypto-currency, I am someone you can trust.*

This philosophy touches everything I do. For example, each morning, when I am doing stretching stuff, just when I start doing upward dog, I look into the mirror and say, *you are the maker of dreams*. But no one likes to say thank you.

4. PEOPLE DIE FROM LIVING

Marlon lived beyond his means. This lifestyle made sense to him. You get more things. You pay for things later. But at some point, you die with a balance due. So, you always come out ahead. Dead people don't have to pay interest. Marlon's wife called it, *kicking the can down the road.* I would ask her what she meant by that, if she would pick up the phone when I called.

So, you can see where this is going. Marlon bought a house for his wife and him, which he couldn't afford. This was a big deal. It was just before that thing happened to their son. I don't know if I should mention that, but if I try not to mention something, it always comes out, so best just to say things. That's another thing I always say: *best just to say things. Then, let the chips fall where they may, blah, blah, blah.*

When Marlon and Viola (his wife's name is Viola) decided to get a house, they started off looking at houses they could afford. But as it turned out, Marlon liked the houses that they couldn't afford more. He would look at the photos of *those* houses, with their swimming pools and giant rooms, and it would make the houses he *could* afford look really bad.

My aunt used to say, "That's true of everything you want. You always want more than you can get." *That keeps you going. Otherwise, you will die.* I added that last bit. I also want to add something else. Here it is: *people die from living within their means.* I believe living within your means is a leading cause of death. I suspect scientific research would confirm this theory, but no one is doing scientific research on this. If they did, they would discover that if you do safe things, and don't do dangerous, stupid things, then you get sad, and then your heart starts to get plaque and stuff, and then you're toast.

Diseases caused by living within your means include but aren't limited to:

Embolisms
Lyme Disease
Ischaemic Heart Disease
Stroke
Chronic Obstructive Pulmonary Disease
Parasitic diseases (tapeworm in particular)
Pneumonia
Tuberculosis
Menopause
Diabetes (type 1 only)
Alzheimer's Disease
Cirrhosis
Lassa Fever
Typhoid
E-coli
Acute Pancreatitis
Dental Abscesses
Atopic Eczema
Rocky Mountain Spotted Fever
The Black Plague
Legionnaires' Disease
Scarlet Fever
Guillain-Barré Syndrome
Acute Appendicitis
Invasive Listeria
Eastern Equine Encephalitis
Balamuthia Encephalitis
Mad Cow Disease
Gallstones
Acute Bacterial Vaginosis (women)
Cholangiocarcinoma

Incontinence
Huntington's Disease
Cellulitis
Erectile Dysfunction (men)
Fibromyalgia
Hepatitis C
Flatulence
Genital Herpes
Scabies
Chlamydia
Lupus
Psychosis
Urinary Incontinence
Verrucas
Lactose Intolerance
and Sunburn.

So, as to living within your means, don't do it. Those of you who have lived within your means and have had any of the above, you know what I am talking about.

5. GETTING IMPORTANT THINGS NAMED AFTER YOU

Marlon bought that house he couldn't afford. It didn't have a pool or giant rooms. But it did have something. *It had a fallout shelter*, which had eighteen-inch thick walls, and lots of canned goods on steel shelves and a Geiger counter, to tell the inhabitants when the nuclear winter was over.

You may not know what a Geiger counter is, but I am in the know about them. Hans Geiger invented it. In 1908. Not a lot of people were really into Geiger counters in 1908, as there wasn't much use for them in the average home. They would become popular later, when people had a need to measure fallout in their homes. Geiger counters could measure Alpha and Beta particles, and later Gamma rays. I have no idea how. I also wouldn't be able to tell an Alpha from a Beta particle, if they were to come up and say, *how do you do?*

My aunt kept telling me things about science, and art and words from foreign languages and philosophies like nihilism and existentialism, over and over again. Existentialism was *au courant* when she was young and in love with someone, which was probably why she wasn't a nihilist. She said lots of valuable things, including stuff about Geiger counters and Alpha and Beta particles and Gamma rays. But I wasn't really listening. She had a tooth that overlapped another tooth in the front of her mouth, and I couldn't understand how she could live with that, knowing people were looking at it. I would kill myself.

So, I was looking at her tooth and not really listening on the day she told me about the gold foil experiment and how later Geiger went back to Germany from England and became maybe a Nazi. Blah, blah, blah. My aunt said that Geiger counters measure in something called Sieverts. Blah, blah, blah. As you read this and sit around doing things, you are getting whacked by about 0.1 micro-Sieverts. Sieverts are named after Rolf Sievert. Do you see the pattern here? If you invent stuff, you get to name things after yourself. Even if you might be a Nazi.

If you go to a dentist and he takes an x-ray, you get 0.4 Sieverts. 100,000 micro-Sieverts, and you get cancer. Outside the Fukushima reactor in Japan, after the third explosion, there were 400,000 micro-Sieverts. If a thermonuclear one-megaton bomb was dropped on an electrical sub-station a mile from your house, it would emit ten thousand times more Sieverts than Fukushima. That's a lot of Sieverts. Which makes you wonder why Rolf wanted the thing named after him.

My aunt would read to me every night, smoking her Gauloises and trying really hard to make me listen. She sometimes talked about a man who didn't come back to see her after they were like dating and in love and whatever. I wasn't surprised, considering the teeth situation. She also made me promise I would be an artist or a writer. Or a physicist, so I could name things after myself. I said, "I promise." She looked at me like I was lying. Then she said, "At least promise not to be a salesman or go into finance or something like that." And I looked right into her eyes, through the cloud of Gauloises smoke and said, "I promise."

Then she shut off the light and went downstairs and played an Édith Piaf record and smoked some more and probably wished that when she woke up, her teeth would be fixed, and that guy would hear about it and come back.

Anyway, I was really impressed by this naming things after yourself phenomenon. I later found out that Mason jars are named after a guy named John Mason. The Jacuzzi is named after the Jacuzzi brothers. The saxophone is named after Adolphe Sax, because he invented it.

My favorite though was Étienne de Silhouette. He was a cheapskate Minister of Finance in France a long time ago, and they named cheap black paintings after him. Not really paintings at all.

You get it. But even a cheapskate like Étienne de Silhouette got something named after him. Still, it's better than Rolf Sievert with all that nuclear fallout stuff. I never had anything named after me.

6. ARE YOU JUST KICKING THE CAN DOWN THE ROAD?

When Marlon and Viola bought their house, the house cost way more than they had. Viola was concerned, but Marlon said, "It actually costs less than you think." Another time Viola said, "Can we afford the house?" And he said, "Yes, we can." Another time, she said, "You aren't just kicking the can down the road, are you?" And Marlon said, "No, I am not." She was okay after that.

Before Marlon and Viola were married, they were dating. If they weren't doing something together, it would be *A BIG DEAL*. Soon, they were at the point in their relationship where they were avoiding big deals. An argument is an example of a big deal. Also, not seeing each other on a Saturday without discussing it first is another example of a big deal.

Once, Marlon went to a football game with Reggie on a Saturday without discussing it with Viola first. He said to Viola afterward, "I didn't think it would be such a big deal."

It wasn't mentioned again. Which was worse. Therefore, it became *AN ELEPHANT IN THE ROOM*.

Big deals become elephants in rooms.

Elephants are pretty benign, by the way. For example, an elephant eats for eighteen hours each day. Which is a lot of time eating, even in places like Italy, where people have long lunches. Italian people's long lunches are nothing compared to an elephant. Elephants ingest two hundred pounds of plants in a day. That's why they sometimes weigh six tons and probably why people started saying you don't want an elephant in your room.

Much later, when they already had many elephants in several rooms (which should have been seen as a bunch of *RED FLAGS*), Marlon and Viola bought that house together for themselves and their two kids. This turned out to be a bad idea. In my opinion, every terrible thing that would occur to them started when they bought that fuckity, fuck, damn house. I didn't know Marlon then. If I did, I might have said something. Blah, blah, blah.

7. SHAMANISM

Way before I came into Marlon's life, I had another investor named David Plaza. I made a pretty good living from David Plaza. Sometimes, I would tell him not to invest. This is *EMOTIONAL INTELLIGENCE* at work. When you tell someone not to do something, they think you care about them. Seriously. I am not making this up.

I would say: "David, don't just go investing, willy-nilly."
It was the sort of thing my aunt would say.
I didn't have parents.
And no one loved me.
Except my aunt.
It seems I was *a risky investment*. As regards love and the like. But she invested in me just the same. Willy-nilly.

Finance is a dark jungle. Full of predators. People will try to get your money. You can lose everything. You need a trusted financial counselor. Someone like me. Wait; you may be thinking: the best thing is not to invest. That's a bad way to think. Risk is fun. Admit it. Closing your eyes (a little) driving in a fast car? Taking a class A drug? Fun. Unlike the previously mentioned living within your means. Deadly.

Sometimes, my investors ask about *THE DOWNSIDE* of risky investments in things like crypto, my specialty. But that's the point, isn't it? It's what makes our hearts beat. It's the adrenalin rush. Here's the thing: when something good happens to us, we just feel dead, right? When we score some big bucks, we feel nothing. Right? Or when we are loved? Nothing. So, you see, it's the downside that makes it fun, not the upside. That's an important lesson I give you for free. It shows maturity to accept the world as it is. This is another example of emotional intelligence.

Another component of emotional intelligence is to let your investor know you're their close friend. People are loyal to their friends and don't go lurching off willy-nilly. You don't want an investor to leave you in the lurch each time they lose money. For example, you tell them to invest in crypto-currency, and they lose their money, and they go lurching off. You must make them understand their unhappiness is not about the money they lost. It's about the empty space they feel inside. That nothing will give them peace. That whoever they love, they will disappoint. So, what does money matter? Let's just have some dangerous investment fun and hold on with white knuckles. I love the term white knuckles. In investment, we say: "If you're not holding on with white knuckles, you aren't playing, and if you don't play, you can't win." Whatever the fuck winning means.

I find it hard getting people to realize you are their good friend as a trusted investment counselor, because people don't trust you. It would be better if I was a doctor. Doctors get a free pass because they can remove major organs, do rhinoplasty, pump a stomach after a class-A drug overdose and save people who have been in car accidents.

Except for doctors, most people don't trust other people. They think there are big secrets that are being kept from them. Like why they feel empty inside and who controls the world financial markets. So, they are always on the lookout for the real truth from someone they can trust. Some people, like my aunt, found the real truth from Kittuke the shaman in Belize. Kittuke said on his YouTube channel that Western medicine is bad and is just there to enrich pharmaceutical companies. He had trouble saying 'pharmaceutical companies' because most of his teeth had fallen out, but that's the price one pays to discover the cure for cancer. Which he had done. Which has been kept from us by 'armicocial comfanies'. For those who searched him out, Kittuke had a medicine he made from a wild jungle radish, and a paste made by crushing several hundred Hemiptera beetles. He mixed these ingredients with milk to make a drink. It was drunk for eight days. It cured all cancers. Except, apparently, the type of cancer my aunt had. Because it didn't cure her.

He felt bad about that, but explained he couldn't give the money back because of all the work required in crushing Hemiptera beetles and marketing costs.

I get not giving the money back. It's a bad business practice. He couldn't stay in business very long if he was giving money back willy-nilly.

I would have made the same decision in his place. However, I probably wouldn't run a business that sells fake medicines to kind women in great pain. That's where our business practices differ.

8. ALL THE LIGHTS ARE ON

In the financial industry, it's good to know when not to say something. This is hard. We like to say things. Like when clients say they have a hot tip about an upcoming movement in CRYPTOCURRENCY, which is my area of expertise, not their area of expertise. It's frustrating hearing non-experts positing opinions. I want to say to them:

1. You are as dumb as a box of hammers. Or
2. You are one French fry short of a Happy Meal. Or
3. You're not the sharpest knife in the drawer. Or
4. You're one shrimp short of a cocktail. Or
5. You're as smart as a stick. Or
6. One sandwich short of a full picnic. Or
7. You're not the quickest bunny in the forest.

But I don't say anything. I don't want them lurching off. No one likes to be told they aren't the quickest bunny in the forest.

9. THE PRE-FORECLOSURE NOTICE

THE PRE-FORECLOSURE NOTICE came through the mail slot along with the Orvis Women's Clothing catalogue, which was free. The people at Orvis Women's Clothing's thinking in this matter is that if you buy something, it will cover the cost of all those catalogues. This is called investing in the future, which is different than future faking and is considered a sound business practice. Viola saw the PRE-FORECLOSURE NOTICE right away, with its big red letters, so Marlon wasn't so good at the secret-keeping thing that day. Usually, he was good at secret keeping. Making sure Viola was only informed on a need-to-know basis to avoid elephants in the room. Also, the phone company had cut off his landline. They did this because he hadn't paid his phone bill. It was on his *to-do list*. He hadn't done it yet.

This could be why he was distracted. He meant to keep an eye out and get to the mail first, around one, when the mail came. Just in case there was something bad like a PRE-FORECLOSURE NOTICE. But he was a little tired and stressed about the whole phone bill thing and was thinking of big ideas and Viola got there first. He said, "Can we talk about this calmly?" They could not. This was another *red flag*.

Next, he did what they call in military circles, *a proportional response*. He walked right into the living room, and he laughed and said *it was all a misunderstanding*. Then he came over all serious and said that he really might change the mortgage company to punish them for their sloppy bookkeeping. Then he laughed some more, as if sharing a private joke with himself, which he had decided to share with Viola.

He had some news. He had had some great financial success in the stock market just in the last few days and hadn't been able to decide how he was going to spend the money. He hadn't told her, because he knew she thought he kicked things down the road, and he wanted it to be a surprise. Now he was thinking he would pay off the mortgage arrears but also pay off the house completely! He said, "Why pay those bad people at the mortgage company more interest?" He would enjoy telling them they had only hurt themselves. She could listen in to the call if she wanted. And, getting all shy and romantic, he said he was going to buy her a new car. Any one she wanted. Within reason. He wasn't made of money.

She didn't say thank-you. She said, "How far behind are we with the mortgage?" He couldn't believe she was still on that subject. He said he was going to pay it off. So, what difference did it make? She was all quiet and staring at him. He realized he had to tell the truth. "Okay," he said, it was "three months." There. He had said it. He had come clean, and now the chips would fall where they may.

Actually, it was a year and a half. But he wasn't going to say that. In military circles, they would have called that *an unwise maneuver.* He had been good at getting the mortgage company to hold off. He had told the mortgage company he had cancer. He had told the mortgage company he had four small children at home who all had asthma. Sometimes, he would send the mortgage company some money, even when he, as he explained, was dealing with his chemo treatments. This bought him a little time.

He told the mortgage company that paying them was more important to him than even getting better from cancer. This was a very powerful thing to say, and he would feel himself welling up, even though he didn't actually have cancer. But after a while they went ahead and sent the PRE-FORECLOSURE NOTICE, having sent warnings already and going to court and stuff like that and then there came that day when Marlon was tired of thinking of big ideas and was slow getting to the mailbox.

To be fair, Marlon couldn't always focus on things like bills. Or getting to the mailbox in a hurry. He was always thinking of new things. Marlon was just one of those guys with lots of ideas. The important thing, as he said to Viola, was that there was trust between them, because a relationship is nothing without trust. So, he hoped he had earned her trust. But what could she do? It's sort of like getting a lottery ticket handed to you. You're not going to win but you're not going to tear it up before they announce the numbers on channel five, are you?

10. GENERAL TSO'S CHICKEN

Three months later, when the actual FORECLOSURE NOTICE came, Marlon was quicker and got to the mail first. This time there was a discount coupon for The Formosa Gardens Restaurant (five dollars off the General Tso's chicken platter), an L.L. Bean catalogue and the FORECLOSURE NOTICE taped to the door. He almost missed it. Despite it being taped. Right there on the door. These notices are magical. When you get them, everything stops. Boom. Colors seem to change, boom, and sounds seem to distort. Marlon was both excited and depressed at the same time.

Then Marlon folded up the FORECLOSURE NOTICE and put it in his back-pocket until he could think of a place to hide it. Then he spent a long time looking at the pictures on The Formosa Gardens Restaurant coupon. He thought the restaurant, in addition to the General Tso's Chicken Platter, the Combination Platter with Shrimp with Lobster Sauce, which included an egg roll and spareribs, looked good. He also thought about other things. Like who was General Tso and why did he get a meal named after him?

11. YOUR ODDS OF WINNING THE LOTTERY

I specialize in some exotic financial instruments.

But also, some simple things like derivatives. Don't worry if you don't know what they are. Do you know how your computer works? Exactly. Derivatives are just a bet on a price. Like betting on a horse.

Then there's leverage. If you leverage your derivative, you can make money much faster. Also, lose it faster. But you will be thinking you are going to make money, which is a more positive way of thinking, so you don't have to worry about the downside.

When David phoned me that day, I thought I could interest him in a cool derivative called *an interest rate swap*. He said no. He wanted me to buy him lottery tickets. I thought that was crazy. He could go to a liquor store and buy them himself. Also, there are those machines where you can use your family birthdays and your lucky numbers to put together a winning combo. He said he wanted me to buy five thousand dollars' worth of lottery tickets for each of the three days each week that there was a Powerball draw for the next three weeks. Forty-five thousand dollars in lottery tickets. He was thinking that buying more lottery tickets would increase his odds of winning the lottery. This was partially true. My business is based on understanding probability. With that many tickets, his odds of winning increased to one in three hundred million. As his investment counselor and his friend, I wanted to convey this to him. I chose my words carefully. I didn't want him to think that I thought he wasn't the quickest bunny in the forest.

Before he phoned, I never really got people buying lottery tickets. Where's the risk? Two dollars? That doesn't get the heart beating. There is no fear in losing two dollars. It's not like driving your car at high-speed and closing your eyes (just for a few seconds). That's exciting. Spending two dollars on a lottery ticket isn't.

I did some thinking on my feet. I said that I would do it for a service charge of ten percent. Also, I would also get ten percent of anything he won. Which was fair.

He said he really wanted to win, which was sweet, **but our desire for something doesn't increase the likelihood we will get it.** You don't have to know anything about probability to know that.

I think his mother told me he was on the spectrum or something and I should look after him and that was probably a factor in my taking on the responsibility of buying the lottery tickets. I offered him the derivative interest rate swap deal a second time, but he really wanted the lottery tickets.

12. SOME SORT OF CRANK

I went to Frank's Wine and Spirits on La Brea and tried to buy twenty-five hundred two-dollar Powerball lottery tickets. A hunched, bald guy, with tufts of hair at his temples, thought I was some sort of crank and said, "Are you some sort of crank or something?" Because he worked in a liquor store, he had met a few cranks. The people who had given up. The ones who realized that the odds were stacked against them. They had become cranks, trying to sell him a story to get one of those little pocket bottles of Seagram's Extra Smooth vodka.

He said again, "Are you some sort of crank?" I told him that I was a professional investment counselor and that I was working for a client. He said, "A client? Do you know what the odds are of winning the Powerball Lottery? Like a million to one. What sort of investment counselor are you?" I didn't correct him. He sold me five hundred tickets. "Good luck," he said. Blah, blah, blah.

I then spent the day buying tickets. I put four thousand dollars in the lottery machine inside Ralph's Supermarket on Sunset. An old woman watched me as the machine printed out every ticket. It took a long time. She was thinking I was some sort of crank.

Eventually, I had a black trash bag full of Powerball tickets.

You can't save people from themselves. This is an important thing that all of us should know. My aunt couldn't save me. But don't blame her.

13. BIG DEALS AND BRAD PITT

Marlon would count the days between his arguments with Viola as if it were a competition. He was very proud when sometimes they would go five or ten or fifteen days. Fifteen days was their record.

They almost didn't get to fifteen days because of the film *The Curious Case of Benjamin Button*. Viola was being a bit of a know-it-all and saying Matt Damon was the star of *The Curious Case of Benjamin Button*, and Marlon said it was Brad Pitt in *The Curious Case of Benjamin Button* and not Matt Damon (like she said). He saw her look it up on her phone and rather than apologizing, she said she was just looking at Instagram. Which wasn't true. She was on Wikipedia. This is the thing about *big deals*. They aren't really *big deals* in the ordinary world.

I mean, who cares who starred in *The Curious Case of Benjamin Button*? (It was Brad Pitt by the way, please don't argue).

Once you are in a relationship, little inconsequential things become big deals because of history. History is all the big deals in a life together, one after the other. When someone brings up something from history, *that's a red flag*.

Film was Marlon's thing. Viola had her things too, and he would give it up in arguments about her things, but film was his thing, and she wouldn't give it up on *The Curious Case of Benjamin Button* issue.

Marlon wondered what would happen if they got to forty-five days.

14. CAN WE TALK ABOUT THIS CALMLY?

It's easier to be sympathetic with someone if you know their back story. That's why in business you don't want to hear their back story. You want people to be a number, or an asset, or a liability. So you can make strategic moves, to maximize your profitability. You don't want to rescue them, or look after them, or pity them, or help them on their way. That's a good way to lose money.

Life is simpler when you don't know anything about people's lives. Better to watch movies or read books. That way you can care about people without it costing you anything.

Marlon knew the score. The mortgage company wanted their money, blah, blah, blah. But still, this time, they had gone too far. All the neighbors could have seen the notice. Taped on their door. It would have been embarrassing. Sure, the mortgage company wanted their money, but shouldn't they still care about him as a person? Didn't they want to know his backstory? They could have spoken on the phone, and he could have explained why he was late. He could have told them the latest on his treatment and would have told them he was part of a promising clinical trial, and about his stock market success, though there still might be a cash-flow issue, but short term and in a few weeks, maybe a few months, they would have been paid.

And were they really going to throw a cancer patient out on the street? In his head, Marlon could accept he REALLY didn't have cancer, but THEY didn't know that, so it was the same thing as throwing a cancer patient out on the street.

It was good Marlon was what is called an *ideas man*. Because right away, he was thinking. His thinking went like this: First, analyze the problem. Okay, here was the problem. The mortgage company said they 'wanted' money. That's where he would start. What had they said, when calmer heads were prevailing? They had said everything would be cool if he would pay 218,000.42 dollars in arrears and penalties. Haaaa. Right there on one of those notices with the big red letters, they should have also printed the laughing/crying emoji. Who has that sort of money?

Marlon reminded himself that you must keep a cool head in a crisis. 218,000.42 dollars *seemed* bad. But to know what a notice like that really means, you must read between the lines. So, he read between the lines. He read it again, slowly and carefully. It turned out to mean the same thing between the lines.

He was so busy reading it and rereading it that he didn't see Viola sneak up and snatch the FORECLOSURE NOTICE and run to the bathroom and lock the door. Then he heard her crying through the door. That made him sad. Had she been strategic, she would have stuck with the crying and made progress.

But then, like a crazy person, for no reason, she completely changed and came out of the bathroom screaming and started breaking things and hit him on the chest, and even on the side of his face. He said, "Can we please talk about this calmly?" Her rage was becoming a real problem in their relationship. Maybe I should get her a book on anger management, Marlon thought.

15. JUST BECAUSE YOU WANT SOMETHING, DOESN'T MEAN YOU GET IT

When I was young, I knew somebody called Michael Allen, who wanted to be successful and would tell me how hard he worked. My aunt would say he was a good example of someone who works hard and a model to all of us, and she looked at me.

I know she was trying to encourage me. But even then, I knew something about probability and just because you work hard and desire something, doesn't mean you will get it. Hard-working Michael Allen wanted to be an actor and a director and work in show business. He read many books on the subject. He appeared in our local community theatre's version of *Wicked*. He went to State College and studied theatre with a minor in filmmaking. After graduating, he went to New York and had an internship at the Circle in the Square Theatre. Then he moved to LA and worked as a PA on little independent films. He borrowed some money and made a short film about a PA who has no money in LA and tries to make a short film about a PA who has no money in LA. It got an honorable mention at the San Francisco short film festival. Then he was out of money and ended up getting a part-time job at T-Mobile on Ventura Blvd in Studio City. Later he became the manager there. So, all that hard work didn't pay off. Unless he secretly wanted to be the manager of a T-Mobile store all along.

I knew another guy, Tom Wilkes, who fell in love with a woman. He really desired her in a big way. He would spend hours gazing at her at work. He also sent her flowers every day, with a new poem each time, that he would write. She finally complained to human resources, so he stopped doing that.

After the flower and poem fiasco, Tom decided he would just stand near her desk and smile at her whenever he had a break. She said that if he kept doing that she would march straight back to

HR, and he would be sorry.

Tom got a special at the Bosley Hair Clinic and got them to fill in the bald spot that he had at the back of his head. He joined a gym and worked out. A guy at the gym told him to take creatine to help build muscle. So, he did. He also went on a diet to lose some weight. Which he did. Not a lot, because it was really hard, but a few pounds. He got a book about how to get a girlfriend called "How to get a Girlfriend." It was self-published on Amazon. The same author had also self-published a book called "How to Keep Clothes Wrinkle-Free (For Travelers)" and another book called, "Simple Lawnmower Maintenance for Non-Gardeners." But his most successful book was "How to Get a Girlfriend." One line in the book said, *Girls like a man with a sense of humor and self-confidence.*

When I saw him by the driveway at the front of my aunt's house (when I was selling it to cover the back property tax and before the Marlon fiasco), he told me how great his desire was for this girl. Her name was Sue Chance. He said, "Sue Chance is the one." And that *he really loved her.* He was *confident* that he would win her over because he wanted her so much. "I am just going to tell her we are going to be together and that's that." And I said, because I know a lot about probability, "What if she doesn't feel as strongly?" And he said: "I have enough love for the both of us." This is a widely held theory, one person having enough love for two people, but it doesn't have a firm statistical foundation. I told him, "There are a lot of fish in the sea," as that's what my aunt would have said. She said those sorts of aphorisms. And my aunt would have told me it was an aphorism. Tom looked at me blankly after I delivered my fish aphorism. As if I had just spoken to him in French. Il y a beaucoup de poissons dans la mer.

I realized later, after the arrest, that Tom believed that if you find your one perfect partner, living will be more tolerable.

Tom decided to ignore the lady from HR and the two notices she had given him, including one that said *FINAL WARNING* on it. Sue was the one. He was going to take the big risk and see the big return. On the big day, he told her he loved her. He walked right up and said to Sue: "I love you." She went to HR, and they fired him and escorted him from the building. So, you see, just because you desire something doesn't mean your odds of getting it improve.

16. LOTTERY WINNER

On day one of David's first five thousand dollars' worth of tickets, his investment produced some winning results. He won six dollars, and he won eighteen replays.

He said, "Now my odds of winning have improved."

No, they hadn't, but there is no explaining probability to some people. People want to believe that their will can triumph over probability. Because they want their will to triumph over everything, including all the things that are inevitable. Statistically, inevitability wins almost every time. That is statistically true, you can look it up.

I bought the next ten thousand dollars' worth of lottery tickets over the next few days, so I was ready for the Wednesday night draw, and the Saturday draw. After the Saturday draw, it took me three days to check all the numbers. I was bored and thought I should throw out all the lottery tickets and just tell David he lost. But then I thought, what if one of these tickets comes in at twenty or thirty thousand dollars. It just goes to show you how infectious this whole hope thing is. Infectious, and a huge time waster. When I think of hope, I think of all the time that people lose hoping.

And then this happened.

I checked another ticket. Fifteen, eighteen, twenty-six, twelve, seventy-eight, and the Powerball number sixteen. I had the California Lottery page on my computer screen. I read the numbers off the screen. Fifteen. Well, that was one of the winning numbers. Okay, a good start. Then I read the next number: eighteen. Okay, at least he was going to get a replay. The next number was twelve. Wow. Money. Like twenty-two dollars. Next number. Twenty-six. I checked again. Yep. Crazy. He was going to win five hundred and forty-eight dollars. Next number seventy-eight. My breath just got short. My skin tingled. I panicked. I don't know why I panicked. But it felt like I was balancing something delicate and dangerous. If you understand the feeling. No logic in it. But terrifying. David would be getting around three hundred and twenty-five thousand dollars.

And then the Powerball.

Sixteen. He got the Powerball.

The world was spinning. I looked at the top of the page. His winning total:

Seven hundred and seventy-two million dollars.

I was thinking, as anyone would, maybe I should keep the ticket and say it was mine. How would he know? Right? I could give him a few million. Maybe ten million. Maybe that would be too much. It would make him suspicious. That would make our relationship complex. So maybe I would give him like twenty thousand dollars. As a friend. That's the sort of thing a friend does. And it wouldn't be a *red flag*.

My aunt would have been disappointed. If I said, "No one will know," she would have replied, "God will know." But when I was ten, she told me she didn't believe in God anymore because of something that happened, which was bad. So, she would not have said, *God will know.* She would have said, "I will know." Which was worse.

On the other hand, and to be fair to me, I had spent a lot of time on these tickets. Also, I chose the stores to buy the tickets and it's not like twenty thousand dollars I would be giving him, willy-nilly, isn't a lot of money. And it's not like he earned it. I did all the work.

It was an accident he won. No skill was involved. Think of all the people who work hard and get very little. Also, think about me. I lost my parents. What do I get for that?

But then something caught my eye. The date. I was tired from checking so many tickets. And I had been looking at the winning numbers.

From the previous week.

It took me a moment to process this. I had the winning lottery numbers, but it was for a different week.

So, it wasn't a winning ticket.

This was unfair.

Or fair.

Or just the nature of things.

The arbitrary nature of, well, nature. If you want to be cared about, get a dog.

David wouldn't be getting anything at all. He just lost twenty thousand dollars, and he didn't even know it.

I thought maybe I could beg the lottery service. It was only one week off. I could point out how unfair it was. That probably wouldn't work. They had heard it all before. From cranks. Maybe I could rub out the date. That had probably also been tried before.

I realized that nothing could be done. No lives would be changed. No fortunes made. No reward for virtue, no reward even for risk, no reward for my hard work and good judgment. My aunt was good and got cancer and died in a filthy hammock in a jungle. So what, right? Lots of good people die. Lots of hard work goes unrewarded. There is plenty of proof the world isn't ordered. So, if you are one shrimp short of a cocktail and you are dutifully waiting your turn to get your just reward, good luck. Nobody cares about fair. Blah, blah, blah.

Ignore me. I am just bitter that I lost seven hundred and seventy-two million dollars minus twenty thousand.

17. LABRADOODLES

Sometimes talking about elephants in the room creates new elephants in the room, particularly if you blame your partner for the elephants being there in the first place. Marlon made a point of not going down this road; Viola, on the other hand, would go down this road.

About Labradoodles for example.

Marlon hoped to get a Labradoodle one day, but Viola only liked dogs from shelters. You rarely saw a Labradoodle in a shelter, because people like them so much. For a reason.

Marlon didn't mind dogs you had to purchase, because if you wanted a Labradoodle, you were going down the purchase a Labradoodle road. But Viola was a bit "know-it-all-y" about shelters and dogs and how there are too many strays and kill shelters and a whole bunch of other dog-related things.

He wanted their latest streak to get past nine days, so when the topic began to become a big deal, he employed a new strategy. He showed her pictures of cute Labradoodles on the internet. She said they were "cute". Not an outright win, but not an outright argument either.

It also made Marlon realize the nuances of arguments. For example, Viola saying: YOU BETTER NOT SAY THAT AGAIN was one type of argument. It required both to remember what they said in the past. They couldn't completely do this as they had so many arguments, they all got muddled. So, if Marlon made a really passionate denial, Viola would sometimes begin to doubt her recollection because of the medications, and it would buy him wiggle room.

Another type of argument would start with Viola saying: YOU BETTER NOT DO THAT AGAIN, MARLON. This was more serious. For example, her saying, "You had better not risk our savings on dangerous investments," is something she was telling him not to DO rather than not to say. There would be evidence if he DID it. No wiggle room. He could be in real trouble.

So, Marlon would keep his financial actions secret and just talk a lot. If he said something wrong, it could be remedied by various practices, like showing Labradoodle puppy pictures. This might also allow him wiggle room to change the subject and argue about something completely different. Marlon thought it was a good life-lesson to recognize that if you can't stop arguing, you can have arguments that have an easier resolution. For example, if you can't get a Labradoodle, maybe you can get a Basset Hound-Pomeranian mix with one eye from a local shelter. You're still getting a dog.

By the way, elephants have some differences. Ear size for example. Also, the head shape; African elephants have flat heads, and Asian elephants don't have flat heads. But these elephant nuances don't matter, because an elephant is still an elephant and they are all basically grey. That made Marlon sad when he thought about it, but he wasn't sure why.

18. A BLEMISH

I think about ownership and theft a lot. Because some people describe me as a thief.

Some people have bad posture, or maybe a blemish. Which gives people an unfair perception of them. "Oh, look at that person, they have a blemish. Ugh." Same with me and the 'thief' thing. Take it easy. Go easy on the judgment thing. Until you have all the facts. I personally think I am the hero of this sordid tale. But you judge. Later, when you know the whole story.

19. NOISSESSOPER

When Marlon and Viola had been living in the house they couldn't afford for some while, and after that whole big tragedy thing, and after the PRE-FORECLOSURE NOTICE thing and then the FORECLOSURE NOTICE thing, and Viola's rage thing, someone came to their house. Marlon was a long way from the front door. He thought he heard something outside but wasn't sure because they lived next to an electrical substation, and there was always a loud humming sound that came from the substation, which sometimes sounded like fifty doorbells all ringing at the same time.

But there was a person at the front door. They rang the bell. Marlon ran to the door and yelled to Viola a few times: "I'll get it. I'm getting it. No, I'll get it." The person who came to the door rang the bell again just as Marlon got there. Marlon looked at him from inside through the sheer curtain, but didn't get too close, so it would seem like no one was home. Which was half-true.

Viola called from the other room, "Marlon, did you get it?" And Marlon said, "Yeah, I got it." And Viola said, "I didn't hear the door open." And Marlon yelled back, because she was at the back of the house near the electrical sub-station, "It was the Jehovah's Witnesses, so I didn't want them to know we were home."

And then the person who had come to the house went away and Marlon crept up to the door and saw that there was something there on the glass, backward. And it said, NOISSESSOPER, which made Marlon open the door.

But Marlon had forgotten that since he had installed the Chubb alarm door sensors, (in a special 'Family Safe' package, which included three movement detectors, and eight window sensors, all for eighteen dollars a month, interest-free for the first six months) the doors would go *beep-beep*, each time he opened a door, as he couldn't figure out how to disable it.

It's funny, Marlon thought, as the door went *beep-beep*, we say disable about official things, like alarms, but with a bathroom tap, we just shut it off. We don't disable it. He had opened and closed the door so quickly, that he had forgotten to get the paper the man had taped to the window. So, he opened the door again.

Beep-beep.

He realized Viola would hear it, so as quick as he could, he grabbed the notice that the guy had stuck on the door with tape. The tape made the notice tear a little when Marlon grabbed it, took it inside and quickly shut the door.

Beep-beep.

He turned the paper over, and it said, REPOSSESSION. Then there were lots of legal this and thats, and therefores and forthwiths. Mentions of the state and the city, and judges, and statutes with numbers. Blah, blah, blah. BOOM. They were coming back at FIVE that day to EVICT THEM. Shit. Poof.

20. SHOW BUSINESS

I realized at some point that people don't do business just to make money. This is a good thing to keep in mind when you are doing business with people. They need other things: attention, love, approval and validation. They will pay for these things, and most of these things don't cost you anything. So, there is a margin for profit here. You see my thinking? Everybody wants to be the star of their own imaginary film. Everyone is sure they are heroes triumphing over insuperable obstacles. As heroes, they figure they are entitled to a little wiggle room. And entitled to a lot of other things. They have suffered more; they have worked harder. They deserve more. It's not about fair, it's about right.

The writer and filmmaker Steven Bernstein, who would be important to Marlon later, would tell a story about a guy who worked as a zookeeper in the elephant enclosure at a zoo. His job was to clean up after the elephants. One day, the elephants all had digestive problems, causing them to have diarrhea. All of them. Spraying everywhere. Even on the zookeeper. By the way, an elephant's stomach is subdivided into four different compartments:

the rumen,
reticulum,
omasum,
and abomasum.

All four of these stomachs were upset in the elephants.

That day the zookeeper went home covered in elephant shit. I am not sure why he didn't change at the zoo, but that would ruin the story. He got home, and his wife looked at him and said: "You are covered in elephant shit. You should quit. And the zookeeper said:

"What, and leave show business?"

21. ALL PROPERTY IS THEFT

Stealing depends on there being ownership.

If something isn't owned, it can't be stolen, right?

If you were a king or queen and you 'stole' something in your kingdom, it wouldn't be stealing. You could call it a tax, or you (in your kingly/queenly capacity) could decide the person who owned the thing you took was a *subversive*. Maybe they were plotting against you! So, you 'seized' the thing in question. Note: seized, not stole.

So, taking something from someone else isn't necessarily theft. Keep that in mind before you start judging me. Next is the whole idea of ownership. Anarchists have thought about this a lot. There's a great expression from anarchists, which is this: *all property is theft*.

There's a problem with lots of cool expressions. Sometimes they are only designed to chant when you're marching and it's not something you can use in your day-to-day ordinary life. For example, 'death to the ruling classes' isn't something you would say in the household goods aisle at Pavilions supermarket.

All property is theft is a good conversation starter if you're looking to start a conversation. Or if you want to seem like a subversive. Not so subversive that you get arrested by a king, but subversive enough that you can get a date with someone who likes subversives.

22. LORD ELGIN AND ONE HUNDRED AND SEVENTY CRATES

Marlon had a lot of junk in his back yard. It wasn't junk to start with. But he would leave things or forget about them or mean to start something and never quite get to it. Boxes, tools. Things. At one point he got a plaster model of the Parthenon. He was going to make it into a cool planter. Viola was dubious but was glad he was going to do something with the back yard. It was built in the 5th century BC and is part of the Acropolis in Greece. The original. Not the model. The model was about six weeks old when Marlon first bought it. Then it was four years old. And green and warped.

Even though I'm selling cryptocurrency, that doesn't qualify me as an anarchist per se.

I do wonder why a person who owns something that someone else doesn't own thinks they are a better person than that other person. Do they think they have been rewarded with a trophy in the better person contest?

If someone has got a trophy for virtuous work, I would get that they have ownership of that trophy because of all their virtue. But if someone is a tyrannical king and just takes things from people and then dies, and those things get passed to the royal great, great grandkids, why is that stolen property sacrosanct? Not trying to get an anarchist to date me, but am I wrong? Do old thieveries become legitimate because of the passage of time?

I will explain why this is important later.

How about countries that go to war and conquer other countries and colonize them and then take things from those countries and put them in museums? Museums are built like churches and people whisper in them like they are there to worship the things they are looking at. This helps with the idea of forgetting they were stolen.

Lord Elgin was famous for stealing things.

He stole them from the most famous building in Greece. The Parthenon. Most thieves don't get to have the things they stole named after them. Lord Elgin was lucky in this respect. His stolen things are called The Elgin Marbles. It's always an honor to have something named after you. They are in room eighteen of the British Museum in London. People whisper when they enter room eighteen. If a school party comes in and gets noisy, their teacher will say *ssshh*, it is a place of worship.

In 1801, when Lord Elgin was the ambassador to the Ottoman Empire (which ruled Greece), he removed a hundred and seventy crates of sculptures and friezes and the like from the PARTHENON, the most famous building in the world. Lord Byron, the poet, said Lord Elgin was 'a dishonest and rapacious vandal'. Rapacious is a word that isn't used as often as it should be nowadays.

The Parthenon is thousands of years old and represents ancient Greece, where democracy started, and stoicism, philosophy (mostly) and anarchy. Though I don't think they came up with the good anarchy slogan, *all property is theft*. But they had the idea. Ex nihilo nihil fit. Which is Latin not Greek. So maybe not theirs. Sometimes, in business, you need audacity. A little promise won't move the needle, but a big one will. Same thing with The Elgin Marbles. A few people taking a few marble centaurs? The Greeks around town might have gone, "Wow! What are you doing there?" But a hundred and seventy crates? It seems sort of official. Forces beyond control. Pretty audacious of Lord Elgin, and a good business practice.

Lord Elgin shipped the marbles to England and then put them in the British Museum. It's been a long time. Thousands of whispering school parties. So, I guess they don't count as stolen anymore. Like my aunt's bracelet. Time has passed. We all have moved on. Ancient history. Things change. Bygones.

Some Greeks don't agree. My aunt probably didn't either. Theft and ownership and rapaciousness are in a big grey area. It's where I live.

23. A LOSER, A FAILURE, A LIAR

When she found out they might be losing their home and Marlon had been lying to her in a big way, Viola told Marlon that he was a loser, a failure, and a liar. Then she said, "*We are going to lose our home*" because of him, and she would "*never, ever, ever forgive*" him, "*ever.*" Or "*believe*" him "*ever again*".

He knew he had to remain calm. She was exaggerating, and she wasn't listening at this minute, because she was being *emotional*. And you can't be emotional in a crisis. So, he had to be strategic. To get her back on board. He told her that this was *crazy* as they were, he paused to strategically read her face, *actually rich*. Which was exceptionally audacious.

Her hand kind of flinched or something. A little jerk. He wasn't quite sure what that meant, but he made his move. He said, "I'm not responsible for the mortgage company's error. Obviously." He also gave her his chin dropped, cute smile thing, which sometimes made her laugh. It should have worked. But something seemed changed about her. Maybe she wasn't feeling well.

24. ICONOCLAST

When Marlon was first dating Viola, it came time to meet her parents, who lived in Encino. Meeting parents, it is generally agreed, is a ritual. Often seen in movies.

It is odd, our relationship with movies. We know they are based on the lives of humans like us. But they aren't us. But they are. People measure themselves against actors, but they feel they are themselves actors performing. Anyway, this is what Marlon felt. Now he had a performance coming up; he was going to play the part of *the really nice guy, with good moral foundation and a steady income. Also tall, aged between twenty-eight and thirty-five* to make a good impression on Viola's parents. There was a problem in that he wasn't tall. The rest he thought he could handle. But where to eat to make a good impression? He chose The Polo Lounge at The Beverly Hills Hotel as the place where they would meet.

The Polo Lounge is a famous restaurant in The Beverly Hills Hotel. Movie stars go there. Which makes it seem real.

Marlon also chose The Polo Lounge at The Beverly Hills Hotel to make him seem like a highflier. Or someone comfortable with the high-flying lifestyle.

He worried about restaurants that have foods that were difficult to pronounce. He remembered his second date with Viola when he had pronounced the 's' at the end of foie gras. Later, in a movie he saw, he heard Jean-Pierre Leaud, who is French, pronounce it correctly. He kicked himself. You don't say the 's'. A lot of people wouldn't be bothered by something like this, but Marlon was not one of those people that wasn't bothered by something like this. He was bothered by this.

Later, he said fraa graa, just in casual conversation, to let Viola know that he knew how to pronounce it. "Hey, Viola," he said, "I wonder why fraa graa isn't more popular in America. It's good."

Marlon wasn't good at pronouncing things. Viola would make

jokes about him not knowing things like how to pronounce things in a gentle, teasy sort of way. Maybe later, the teasing would be a big deal, and they would argue about it, but for now, the teasing was okay. Kind of. It did bother him more than he said. He thereafter tried to learn big words. For example: *Iconoclast*.

One time, Viola teased him when he mispronounced something. At first, he laughed, then said he didn't care. He mispronounced it because he was an iconoclast. Pronunciation and knowing which fork to use were *bourgeois* concerns. He made a point of not saying the 's' at the end of bourgeois.

He was worried Viola's parents would:

1. See right through him.
2. See that he was a fraud.
3. Know that he mispronounced words.
4. Know that he wasn't sophisticated.
5. Know that he wasn't rich.
6. Think he was a loser.

He came in once when Viola was speaking to her mom, and she was saying that Marlon wasn't doing well in business, and he didn't have a lot of money.

Later, he said, "Hey, could you not tell your mom that?"

And she said, "Why not? Everybody goes up and down in business."

And he said, "You don't understand."

25. JUST AN OVERSIGHT

Later, Marlon left the door to the fallout shelter/office/man cave open. This was an unwise maneuver. As the phone had also been disconnected again on this particular day (Marlon explained it was a regular technical problem and he was so angry he was thinking of changing providers), Viola had come down looking for him and saw the REPOSSESSION NOTICE. Right there on his desk. When he came home, she called Marlon a loser, a failure and a liar, so it was clear to Marlon he had to alter his strategy. The ability to pivot is a sign of good leadership. He got all serious. And he spoke slowly to demonstrate it was a big confession. He said, *yes*, he had *many faults*. She was *right to be angry*. He was *so ashamed*. But really, it was just an oversight. He was *maximizing his profitability* and was so *into the big picture long term*, he'd *foolishly overlooked the mortgage payment*. He was a *bad person*, and he couldn't *forgive himself for this oversight*. He was just *so busy*, with *so many things on the go, so many things that were really going to pay off in the long term*. He was *certain*, she *would see*.

He could see she was upset so he would *make it right* and he was *going downstairs to the fallout shelter/office/man cave right now*. And he was going to *pay it all off*. And for her patience, he was going to buy her a car. Yes, he already said that, but this car was even better than the one he promised earlier. This one was a white Audi S4. He was hoping this would make her feel better. So, he said again, *a white Audi S4*. Attention to detail helps make people believe you.

She surely should be pleased that she was getting a car. He couldn't prioritize that just now, but at least she knew it was coming. He didn't say that out loud. He didn't have time to explain his plans. He would have to figure that out. Also, he would have to exercise some financial management. A penny saved is a penny earned. For starters, the phone bill. Not the one already cut off.

He would get to that later. But he was still paying for his son's line. Which was pointless.

Viola paused her loser, failure, liar speech to listen. So maybe the car thing had worked. Or maybe she was exhausted. Or maybe it was because of the kids. They had had two kids together. Having kids together gives you leeway in moments of marital crisis. Also, there was that awful thing. That had happened. As angry as Viola was, there was that, and it connected them. It would forever connect them. In a bad way. But still.

26. DELICATE NOTES OF RASPBERRIES THAT FORM IN THE NOSE

Marlon drove to The Polo Lounge to look at the menu a week before the big dinner. So that he could research the food and know how to pronounce it.

He found a book about how to choose wine. It was called *Welcome to Wine: An Illustrated Guide*.

He made a list of twenty good wines. With brief descriptions from the book. For example, *this wine has meaty, red fruit aromas, or this other wine has intense black fruit flavors, or this wine has delicate notes of raspberries that form in the nose*. He repeated those phrases while he drove and wrote them down with a pen, as that is a good way to learn things.

He was amazed at the prices at The Polo Lounge of some of their wines. One wine, a Syrah from Sine Qua Non Winery in the Central Valley cost four hundred and twenty-six dollars a bottle. Marlon thought it must have plenty of meaty fruit aromas at that price. Who would pay that much for a bottle of wine? He was thinking more in the region of twenty-eight dollars. This was a concern.

Maybe he had chosen the wrong restaurant.

He had a fantasy where he lectured to Viola and her parents about wine at dinner and made a good impression. Maybe he could memorize the introduction to *Welcome to Wine: An Illustrated Guide*. Then he thought that was a bad idea. Viola knew he didn't know anything about wine. She would know he was BSing and maybe figure out he was just quoting the introduction to *Welcome to Wine: An Illustrated Guide*.

So even if he made progress with her parents, he would lose ground with her.

He remembered she would drink wine sometimes. Once, when they went out, she ordered it by the glass. "Just the house white, please." So, he had to be careful as she seemed to know something about wine. This is the problem with going out with your girlfriend's parents and your girlfriend at the same time. Consistency.

During his preparation for the big dinner, he parked with the valet one time at The Polo Lounge at The Beverly Hills Hotel, and they charged thirty-five dollars. Not including the tip!

That is probably why they charged four hundred and twenty-six dollars for a bottle of Syrah from the Sine Qua Non Winery. To make it proportional. It was a test. If you are willing to have someone move your car six feet for thirty-five dollars plus tip, then four hundred and twenty-six dollars for a bottle of wine might seem a bargain. But it wasn't really a bargain, Marlon thought. It was just a bottle of wine. To be fair, a wine with a meaty aroma and delicate raspberry notes that form in the nose. Or peppery and floral with notes of licorice. All the descriptions were blending together. He couldn't remember. Which made him panic a little.

The second time he went to The Polo Lounge, he parked at the top of a steep hill near the hotel. Parking is difficult in Beverly Hills, so he was a long way away. It was hot, and he had to walk all the way down the hill and then up the long, curved driveway to the front of the hotel. He went through the lobby of the hotel, turned right and went to The Polo Lounge. They asked if he had a reservation and he said, "No, I just want to look at the menu." And the guy at the desk said, "You were here the other day, and you just wanted to look at the menu then also." Marlon wasn't sure about the regulations about things like this, so he said, "No, that must have been someone else." He was playing it safe.

Marlon studied the menu for over an hour and got several funny looks from the guy at the desk and then some funny looks from some of his colleagues, who the guy must have spoken to behind Marlon's back. Apparently, a lot of people didn't do prep work for their important meals.

When Marlon got back to his car, there was a hundred dollar ticket under his windshield wiper. It was street sweeping day on that side of the street. He folded the ticket several times and hid it in his pocket. He didn't want Viola to see it. It would be a big deal.

When Marlon went back to The Polo Lounge the third time, he decided to pay the thirty-five dollars. He thought the valet had a smirk on his face when he gave him his car. Probably, the guy at the desk had said something smirk-inducing to the valet about Marlon. They must have all known each other.

When Marlon went to the desk at The Polo Lounge, the same guy from before was there. He also seemed to be smirking. It was a different smirk than the valet, but he might have just been a more practiced smirker. He handed Marlon the menu and the wine list without Marlon even asking. Marlon sat with the menu for a bit and then said in a big voice, because he was a long way from the smirking guy at the desk, "I have reservations for Saturday. For four people."

"Yes sir," the guy at the desk said. But he still seemed to be smirking. Maybe it wasn't to do with the reservations. Maybe it was to do with the thirty-five-dollar parking fee and the four hundred and twenty-six dollar bottle of wine. Maybe he smirked at everyone.

27. JOHN WAYNE'S EAU DE TOILETTE

As the big day approached, there was the issue of what to wear. Viola said her dad was tall. Marlon wasn't tall. He wanted her parents to think he was a catch. So, he put a folded sock inside each shoe to make himself taller. He almost slipped out of the shoes a few times on account of the folded socks. He hoped her dad would see him as masculine and they'd have a firm handshake and look at each other eye to eye.

He also wanted to smell good. He used *Calvin Klein Eternity for Men* Eau de Toilette. He put it on his wrists and on his neck. He wasn't sure whether it was too strong. He couldn't really smell it, so he sprayed on a little more. He also sprayed it in the air and walked through it like he had seen someone do in a movie. A newer movie. John Wayne, for example, wouldn't walk through a cloud of *Calvin Klein Eternity for Men* Eau de Toilette.

As they walked out, Viola said, "Whoa, what's that smell?" Later, to make him feel better, she said, "I never realized how tall you are."

28. IGNORE THIS SIGN

Paradox was one of my aunt's words. It seemed to make her sad when she mentioned it, for some reason. She had a big sign up in her room that said, IGNORE THIS SIGN. That was a *paradox*, she said. Also, she said to love someone and, in doing that, hurt yourself; that's a paradox. She thought about lots of paradoxes.

29. TAMING THE TIGER WITHIN

Okay, the repossession was a crisis. No question. But crises must be addressed with ideas and Marlon was, he reminded himself, *an ideas man*. The ideas were really coming to him now. This is what happened when Viola gave him space. Usually, she just couldn't control herself. He had urged her to work on this and had given her a self-help book called: *STOP THE RAGE: TAMING THE TIGER WITHIN, to help her control her rage*. But the day he gave her the book was the day of their biggest argument. She just wouldn't acknowledge that she was part of the problem. He said, "You are part of the problem." He said this in a really calm, therapeutic voice that he had practiced, and it turned out this made her even angrier.

She said, "You're the problem, you asshole, with your lying and your crazy schemes." She wasn't even trying. "You aren't trying," he said in the same therapeutic voice, and she threw a glass at him. He was an expert in her moods and could see the rage coming again like a wave. Also, the thrown glass was also a tip-off.

He was right. She screamed at him, really loud, even louder than the buzzing from the sub-station, which was right next to that part of the house. Then she said it again. That he was a *liar*. He hated when she said that. And she knew he hated it, and she said it anyway to push his buttons. It made him angry, even though she was the one with the anger problem issue. Anyway, he knew, in his heart, he was a good person. Okay, he lied, but he wasn't dishonest. Dishonest was different. Dishonest people tell the truth all the time. Which can appear to the onlooker to be honest, but it isn't. Because they wanted you to trust them, so they could get something from you later. Love, money, something. Marlon knew he was going to do great things for a lot of people. Later. That was his plan. He would fantasize about it. Even things for people who didn't like him. Just to see the look on their faces. But first, he had to focus on the foreground issue. This was good leadership. You must deal with the cards you are dealt. When you are on a sinking ship, you might say you have cancer, or four kids with asthma, to get on a lifeboat. Once the ship sinks and you are safe, you can look around and say, "*I am really sorry,*" to the other survivors. They will forgive you. You are all survivors, after all. Survivors understand survivors and what it takes to survive. They don't want something from you later; they already got what they needed.

Viola was still shouting. When she was like this, she was hard to be around. He wished she had at least read a few pages of *STOP THE RAGE: TAMING THE TIGER WITHIN*.

30. KILLER SCRIPT

On the night of the big dinner, Marlon decided he was not going to pay the thirty-five-dollar parking fee at The Polo Lounge. He decided he would park even further away than last time, two and a half miles away on a side street off Benedict Canyon Drive. Then, he would phone a cab to take them the rest of the way. He thought this a brilliant plan. Viola asked why they didn't use Uber from the house and Marlon didn't want to say. He didn't want to use Uber, because Uber would use his credit card, and he was worried he wouldn't have enough money for dinner.

The cab driver spoke to them right away. He said he wasn't really a cab driver. He was a screenwriter. He asked if they were in show business or the film industry, as he had a screenplay that was a winner. Marlon said, "not directly" and was more "in finance" and Viola said she worked with children with special needs. The driver nodded. He waited a little and then the driver asked Marlon if he had financed films ever, as he really did have a killer script. Marlon said, "Well if you have a script with you, I could take it to some people that I know." Viola looked at him like, *what?* The driver reached backward and handed Marlon his script. Then the driver said, "I really should have you sign an NDA, but I don't have an NDA. So, I will have to trust you. But I registered it with the WGA, anyway, so it's cool." Marlon said, "It's always a good idea to register with the WGA." Viola looked at him again. Then she said, "What is the WGA?" Marlon looked out the window as if he was thinking about something else. Then Marlon said, "It's just film stuff. Reggie is involved. The WGA, the whole nine yards. Big time." He was hoping Viola would drop the WGA thing. They both knew this was becoming a big deal, so they stopped talking, even though the driver was still talking. "You are going to love the script," he said. "It's going to win awards."

They saw her parents waiting by the big floral arrangement near the entrance to The Beverly Hills Hotel, where The Polo Lounge is. As Marlon and Viola got out of the old cab, the valet who made the snide smile at Marlon on his last visit, opened the door for them. "Good to see you again," he said to Marlon, snidely. At least Marlon thought it was snidely. Marlon just knew that Viola was going to ask how the valet knew him. So, before she could ask the question, he strode over to her dad in a masculine fashion and extended his hand.

Marlon said to Viola's father, "A great pleasure to meet you, sir," and Viola's dad (Charles), said, "Very nice to meet you too."

They had a medium firm handshake of medium length.

Viola thought it was wrong that Marlon wanted to please her parents so much. She also thought there was a problem generally with his desire to please people. She thought pleasing people all the time was dishonest. Marlon couldn't get his head around this. There are many advantages to pleasing people. Here are a few:

1. If you please a person, they're not gonna be angry with you.
2. If you please a person, they're not gonna punish you.
3. If you please a person, they might help you.
4. If you please a person, they might like you.

Viola's philosophy was to tell people the truth, which is a risky strategy in business, for example. Using her philosophy, you might tell a friend they don't look good in that dress they just bought. Or when someone gives you a script, you might say you don't have any money to invest in a film. Or later, if you have taken the script and the writing is bad, you might tell them *they shouldn't give up their day job*. Which would make them feel bad. No one wants to hear they shouldn't give up their day job if they don't like their day job and if they really want to be a famous writer. So, her honesty philosophy thing had consequences that perhaps she wasn't considering.

This was different from Marlon. Marlon maybe wasn't wholly truthful with the cab driver. He didn't say, 'Don't give up your day job', and maybe, yes, the cab driver thought Marlon was in film finance, if not *directly*. Later, when Viola and Marlon argued about it, he said, "What is wrong with that? Now the cab driver has hope. Hope is nice."

31. YOU WILL BE SORRY

Marlon and Viola had bought the house they couldn't afford from an old couple. When they visited the house and met the old couple, Marlon tried to *turn on the charm*. But the old couple didn't seem charmed. The old woman never looked at him. She was packing her thimble collection, carefully wrapping each thimble, but first looking at each one. Maybe she was thinking of some memory. But also, she was falling asleep, sometimes. Old people do that, fall asleep in the middle of things. Maybe it's the memory thing. Maybe having lots of memories makes you sleepy. Or sometimes angry. Or sad. Like my aunt, with her paradoxes. And someone on the outside looking at an old person, just thinks, *what a crazy, old person.*

The old man kept saying under his breath, "You will be sorry." The realtor explained he didn't mean the house. When Marlon went downstairs with the realtor to the fallout shelter, the old man wouldn't come. He just said again, "You will be sorry." He said it louder this time, which made the realtor smile but in a kinda nervous way. The realtor said, "He just says that. He doesn't mean the house."

Viola tried to speak to the old woman. "Do you collect thimbles?" The old woman didn't answer. Even though she was awake at that moment. Meanwhile, downstairs in the fallout shelter, Marlon knew he had to get this house. He asked the realtor the price again, and the realtor said the price. Marlon said, "Is that all?" Marlon looked at the realtor's face from the corner of his eye. The realtor seemed impressed.

The old man yelled down the stairs. He had a surprisingly loud voice for an old man. He yelled, "You will be sorry!" There was a shelf of books in the fallout shelter. It turned out that the old man was an avid reader about the coming nuclear war with Russia, and more recently, alternatively China. Or Iran.

The other books on the shelf included: *How to Win Friends and Influence People* by Dale Carnegie. Marlon wondered who the old man was going to be friends with and influence while underground after a nuclear war. The old man had installed the fallout shelter in 1961 and stocked it with canned goods. Also, a lot of potassium iodide tablets. Which you need, to protect your thyroid, which absorbs radioactive iodine, of which there would be a lot in the event of a nuclear attack from Russia, China or Iran.

Nuclear attacks are bad in many ways. Yes, you have your thyroid/iodine issue, but then you also have your Alpha and Beta particles. Alpha particles are bad when inhaled and will damage cells inside you. The good news is they can't really get through your skin. But the breathing problem is a big one. You can't hold your breath for a whole Iranian nuclear attack.

The holding breath scenario isn't much good anyway, because then there are Beta particles, and they can get through your skin. But the really bad news? Gamma rays. They can pass right through clothing and skin, and bones and teeth and everything. They can destroy your cells, mutate your genes and give you cancer. They are super powerful.

So, if you are going to build a fallout shelter, you will want to reduce Gamma rays by one thousand and fifty times. That's a lot, one thousand and fifty times. So, imagine how strong those Gamma rays are to start with. You definitely don't want to be on the street, or in a park, or in a Jacuzzi during a nuclear attack and get hit by Gamma rays. The old man's fallout shelter reduced the Gamma rays by more than one thousand and fifty times. So, it was up to snuff.

It didn't say that in the realtor's particulars, which just said:

GREAT OPPORTUNITY - PRICE REDUCED

An unusual feature is the home's real MID-CENTURY FALLOUT SHELTER, which can be converted into a family recreation room or used as a guest bedroom, with a bathroom en-suite.

It also had a blast door, a generator, a tank for two hundred and seventy gallons of spare water and a transistor radio, so you could hear the all-clear when the nuclear apocalypse was over.

Marlon fell in love with this house because of the fallout shelter. This happens all the time. People say when looking at a house, oh good roof, or, *wow-e-wow honey, look at these huge walk-in closets*. But it's the little things that sell them. Like an electric blind that goes up and down, electrically. Or in Marlon's case, eighteen-inch thick walls in a fallout shelter that stops Gamma rays and has a built-in Geiger counter that will let you know when it is less than one hundred thousand micro-Sieverts outside.

The old woman finally looked at Viola and said: "I don't even like the fucking things." She had picked up one of the thimbles. "You're trapped by your own life. You have done it for so long you can't just throw it away. That's why we do half the things we do. Because we have already fucking done them." Then she went back to packing the thimbles.

Later, Marlon and Viola bought the house they couldn't afford from the old couple. The old woman left Viola one silver thimble with a note: *So you can start your collection.* The old man left a note as well, but for Marlon: *You will be sorry.*

32. A GOOD IMPRESSION

Judy was the name of Viola's mother. Judy kicked off the conversation. She said, "Wasn't the parking expensive?" Viola said that they had parked two and a half miles away so they wouldn't have to pay the parking. The idea was that her parents wouldn't know this. That's why it was a good plan. Now, it wasn't a good plan. Now, he wasn't making a good impression.

It was her tell-the-truth thing in action. Charles gave Marlon a funny look and then Judy gave him a funny look. It was like coordinated funny looks. They weren't smirky looks, which was good, but they were funny looks for sure. Marlon wished Viola hadn't mentioned the far-away parking. But Marlon and Viola were on a thirteen-day streak, so he didn't say anything to Viola about her tell-the-truth thing sabotaging his good impression thing.

They were at the desk in front of The Polo Lounge where they check reservations. Marlon's mind was wandering. The guy behind the desk was the same guy as before and was looking at him. Marlon was wondering why he was looking at him. Was it because he recognized him as the 'just looking at the menu' guy?

Marlon decided not to make eye contact with Viola for a little while. He really loved her. But he wished she hadn't told her parents about the parking plan.

Marlon noticed things had gone quiet. Everyone was looking at him.

And the name on the reservation? The guy behind the desk said, apparently for the second time.

"Oh. It's Marlon," Marlon said.

The guy behind the desk looked at his screen like he was doing security clearance for The White House or something. *Just because you charge four hundred and twenty-six dollars for a bottle of wine doesn't make you more important than me*, Marlon thought. Charles smiled at his daughter like Marlon not realizing he was supposed to give his name was some sort of inside joke. Like Charles was about to tell Marlon not to give up his day job. Judy gave Marlon a reassuring smile, which was nurturing and worse. Marlon felt like a loser. He wanted to show he was substantive, but he was daydreaming. *Damn*, he thought. *What was I thinking? I was thinking about Viola telling her parents about the parking. Why did she do that?* They sat down.

Charles asked Marlon what he did for a living. Right away.

Oh God, thought Judy, *please don't say anything about what you hope to do, young man.* She had learned that Charles wasn't a fan of hope. Hope was impossible with Charles. If you wanted to give up on hope, all you had to do was speak to Charles for five minutes. If you wanted to give up on life, live with him for twenty-five years. He cared about practical things. Money, 401ks, extending the lease on their SUV. *The real world,* Charles called it. Judy had come to learn that *the real world* was a world that didn't have hope or dreams.

"I am in finance," Marlon said. "Pretty small stuff right now, but I have big dreams, right? High hopes. I have some partners, and we are doing some interesting things. Indirectly some show business things. Maybe film stuff. We are deciding." Viola seemed to be drinking from her glass for a long time.

Film stuff?

Oh God, thought Judy.

33. A CHEEKY MERLOT

Marlon was wondering whether he should get a starter.

If he got a starter and a main course, and everyone did that, because he did that, he might not have enough on his card to pay for the meal. He decided not to get a starter.

Then Charles said, "Let's get a bottle of wine."

Okay. Marlon planned for this. There was one wine that he could afford, particularly if he didn't get a starter. Marlon said, "That cheeky Merlot looks good."

Charles said, "Why is it cheeky?"

Marlon didn't know. He had read it in Wine Connoisseur magazine. There was just a long silence. Charles gave him a look as if to say, are you one of those people that strings people along with hope? Are you a bullshit artist? Do you not live in the *real world*?

Marlon didn't remember a lot about the rest of the meal. Judy said she wasn't very hungry.

Also, Viola only had a salad without croutons. Charles said, "Should we get another bottle of wine?" But no one else wanted one. So, they didn't get one. Charles said, "Well, I can't drink it all myself, can I?"

Marlon felt he wasn't making a good impression. Why had he said that stupid thing about what he *hoped to do*? That was a tactical error. Anyone can talk about what they hope to do. A person of substance has done stuff already.

Marlon suddenly said out of nowhere, "If you think hiring experienced people is expensive, try hiring inexperienced people." Charles gave Marlon a confused look and Judy gave Marlon a confused look and Viola gave Marlon a confused look. Actually, Viola's look was more one of horror.

Marlon was trying to demonstrate his business acumen. "I mean in business generally; don't you think, Sir?" Charles wasn't following. Marlon turned to Viola. "I mean, Viola, do you find this to be true at your school?"

Viola said, "Yes, I guess so."

He had saved the situation. He was glad he hadn't said, *Life is hard, but it's better than all the alternatives,* which was on his list of things to say. Also:

1. Run it up the flagpole.
2. Don't give up the day job.
3. Do we have enough bandwidth?

These are the things Marlon figured *experienced businessmen* said, which showed that he had been *around the block,* and *it wasn't his first rodeo.*

Later, when they were leaving, Charles and Judy didn't know that Marlon was right behind them and Charles said something to Judy. He either said looser or loser. Marlon couldn't be sure. Or regarding what. He hoped it wasn't him, as he now felt that he had saved the day and had made a good impression. Judy turned suddenly and seemed maybe embarrassed. Which might have been a tip off. But Marlon couldn't be sure. "You smell lovely," she said. "What is it?" "Calvin Klein Eternity for Men," Viola said. Marlon wished she hadn't. "Christ," Charles said. "And you're taller than I imagined," Judy said.

Viola and Marlon's cab drive back to their car was a catastrophe. They couldn't remember where they had parked the car. They argued about it. *Poof.* There went thirteen days of hard work. *Poof.*

Then they stopped arguing for a while. They found Marlon's car. The meter said over a hundred dollars. Viola had that with her. She said very quietly, "It would have been cheaper, maybe, to park at the restaurant." Marlon knew this.

Marlon was worried she was thinking he was a bullshit artist.

He started the car and turned down the hill, and for some reason, she put her hand on top of his. He looked at her and she had tears in her eyes, and she had a small smile.

She said, "You don't have to impress my parents, but I so love that you wanted to. I love that you tried so hard to make the night special. I love you. You try so hard all the time, and even when you get it wrong, maybe especially when you get it wrong, you seem so small, so desperate, but so sweet. And so anxious to make me happy." Then she really lost it, sobbing and so forth. Marlon was crying too, but possibly because everyone at The Polo Lounge now knew he wore too much *Calvin Klein Eternity for Men* Eau de Toilette. After that, they drove in silence for a while as she looked out the window at the grand houses of Beverly Hills.

Marlon said: "We will live here one day. In a really big house. We can invite your parents over."

She didn't respond until they turned east on Sunset and then she said, almost to herself and with a sad smile, "A cheeky Merlot."

34. WHAT WE COVET AND WHAT WE DESERVE

My aunt, who wanted me to understand the value of a dollar, would give me an allowance.

Not so much money that I could just spend it willy-nilly. But something.

There was a model helicopter that I coveted that was not an ordinary model helicopter. It was three feet long and all the parts could come out, even the engine. So, you could really see what the inside of a helicopter was like. Also, there was a pilot and copilot you put in seats. It was called the Remco Whirlybird US Airforce Rescue Corps helicopter. In my imagination, I could see myself holding it in the air and going, *clickity chickity chickity chickity.* Those are helicopter noises.

It cost fourteen dollars, which was nearly three weeks' allowance. So, I couldn't buy it, willy-nilly.

The man who owned the toy store that stocked the Remco Whirlybird US Airforce Rescue Corps helicopter was called Mr. Liebowitz.

The Remco Whirlybird was at the back of his store. The back of the store had very narrow aisles and lots of boxes of models on the shelves. Mr. Liebowitz didn't like when the kids came in. They didn't buy things.

Mr. Liebowitz preferred to spend his time speaking to old model makers. They talked to each other like they were at a convention of important scientists, comparing their research. They talked about the various techniques and types of paints and glues and things.

I am not a bad person.

I noticed that he couldn't see what I was doing in the back aisles, particularly when he was talking to important model makers. The Remco Whirlybird US Airforce Rescue Corps helicopter had a little

Scotch tape on its box that held it shut. Also, a cool photo on the box top of the copter in action in some war somewhere. Probably Vietnam. I discovered through research that I could remove the tape that held the box together and open it and look inside. Then, I could see the different parts and move them around.

Maybe I was an anarchist? That might give you a different view of my actions. Just because you don't at the time know what an anarchist is, that doesn't mean you aren't one. I might have also been a subversive.

Mr. Liebowitz wasn't nice, and how we treat not-nice people has different criteria than how we treat nice people. Also, I had to be responsible with the money that was given to me, so I understood the value of a dollar. I was a good person, and my intentions in the long term were certainly to repay Mr. Liebowitz. If you can afford the thing you are stealing, it isn't stealing, particularly if you are going to pay it back later.

I discovered that I could just reach into the box and take out a few parts of the unmade model and even hold them up and go: *clickity chickity chickity chickity.*

Mr. Liebowitz didn't even notice.

Even when I put a propeller blade in my pocket.

It wasn't a big moment. I just did it. It wasn't like crossing the Rubicon. It wasn't a hundred and seventy boxes of giant marbles. It wasn't like I was stealing from a king. It was just a Remco Whirlybird propeller blade.

I put the Scotch tape back and sealed the box and as I was leaving, Mr. Liebowitz yelled after me: "Maybe next time you buy something," which sounded kind of nice in his funny, foreign accent. He didn't know what I had in my pocket; he just thought I was one of those damn kids that didn't buy anything.

My aunt said he had been in a concentration camp or something, which was different from the camp I went to for two summers called *Camp Wild Pony.*

35. TURNING ON THE CHARM

On the same day that Viola later found out that their house was being repossessed, Marlon was in his fallout shelter/office/man cave. His computers were set up with two screens on a desk, so he could monitor his stock investments. But he hadn't made any yet, so, he hadn't made any trades yet, or losses, or profits, or really bought or sold any shares.

Once he started trading, he knew, intuitively, it would be something he would be good at. But he hadn't had the capital yet to start properly, and it frightened him a little, but he wouldn't tell anyone that he was frightened. And he was still doing a lot of research.

The lack of profits from the stocks he hadn't yet invested in was why he hadn't paid the mortgage. It was a bit of a paradox. He would think about this for long periods, while watching the financial channels. There were many good ideas for investments on the financial channels and he would write them down for later.

He had a Samsung eighty-five inch big-screen television installed on the wall. He had bought it at Best Buy on the last day of the Geek Squad Smart Deals Sale. He got it just in time. Before the price went up again. Still, it was very expensive, but he didn't have to pay an instalment for the first three months. And there was a free delivery and installation.

The delivery guy who delivered the Samsung eighty-five inch big-screen television finally got it down the narrow stairs with his junior assistant, who he was training. When they had it mounted on the wall, the delivery guy looked all around and said to Marlon, "What *is* this place?" And Marlon said, "A fallout shelter." Because the trainee was there, the delivery guy just said, "Cool." But the trainee said, "What's that?" And Marlon said, "A Geiger counter." And the trainee and the delivery guy nodded like they understood.

Marlon gave them some 1960's vintage canned goods. He gave the delivery guy a can of 1959 Campbell's Pork and Beans and the trainee a can of Cento Jumbo Pitted Ripe Olives. Marlon didn't like olives. The Cento Jumbo Pitted Ripe Olives can was from 1963 and it was dented, so Marlon hoped the trainee wouldn't get botulism or something. But probably he would just put it on a shelf for people to look at it. And then the delivery guy and his trainee left.

Marlon had three other TVs on the walls, which were always on the news channels or the financial channels, because he was in finance. He had a heavy punching bag and some boxing gloves. He had a big television monitor linked to the security cameras he had set up all around the house, in case anyone tried to break in and steal things.

It also meant he could see the mailman at the front door and the neighbors outside, see his wife in different rooms, and the hallway that led up to the fallout shelter, and even himself. He could see himself looking at himself looking at the monitor with the security cameras.

On this particular day, he could also see that his wife was still upstairs, yelling and throwing things. But he couldn't hear her. That was surreal. Then he saw her coming down the hall to the fallout shelter/office/man cave door on security camera number four pointed at the door to his fallout shelter/ office/man cave. Camera number five pointed at the sad, dark room.

When Viola was right outside the blast door, Marlon could see her lips moving but still couldn't hear anything. There was an inspection hole that went through the door. It was there so that after the apocalypse, you could see who was outside knocking, begging for mercy. They put things like inspection holes in blast doors before they had invented security cameras. No way Alpha or Beta particles could get down that hole. But Gamma rays were a different story. While Gamma rays were around, better if you didn't know who was outside your fallout shelter begging for mercy. Anyway, if the people outside were bombarded with Gamma rays, they were toast.

Viola knew that Marlon couldn't hear through the eighteen-inch thick walls, so she figured she should yell through the inspection hole. Marlon could just about hear her. But she was still muffled. Then she went away. But she was technological. So next, she used Facetime to connect with the big screen. Right there in his fallout shelter, her image was giant on the screen. He could hear her on the surround sound speakers and the big sub-woofer. *This was his last chance*, she said. And she meant it.

Marlon gave a big smile and a thumbs-up. He was turning on the charm. Then she shut off her camera. Marlon was a little sad. The pressure wasn't helping, but it wasn't her fault. Marlon thought about one of those motivational videos he watched, and he took a deep breath and said: *I got this.*

36. A PROPOSAL

He started to work. The first thing he did was check his bank account. It came up on his computer screen. $4,200.00. He went over to a big whiteboard he had hung on one wall and wrote $4,200.00. Above that, he put what he owed to the mortgage company. $213,800.42. He subtracted what he had from what he owed, leaving $213,800.42 to raise.

He had a very large clock on another wall from an old train station. It was very big. And it worked. It was nine-thirty in the morning. Marlon thought, *Okay. Okay. Okay. Here we go. We can turn this around. Boom.* Everything was on the table. *Boom.* He had until five that afternoon to raise two hundred and thirteen thousand, eight hundred dollars and forty-two cents. *Boom, boom.* Plenty of time. Two hundred and thirteen thousand, eight hundred dollars and forty-two cents. *Boom.* He felt hot. The air-conditioning wasn't working well. He did a little shadow boxing. He did some burpees. He was getting into the game. He talked to himself: *You can do this.* He took a big breath. *Let it out.* Then another big breath and he phoned the mortgage company to get more time.

He had done it before. He could do it again. *Be strong. Be confident. You set the agenda, not them.* And *boom.* There they were on the phone. He was through to them. He was charming, vulnerable, funny. He called them by their first names. It's always good to call people by their first names. So they know you know they are human after all, with legs and arms, and a backstory and a first name.

He had a proposal. To everyone's benefit. They listened. Or seemed to be listening, but you're not really listening if you already know what you are going to say. And it was obvious to Marlon they weren't listening, when they *took a tone*. They reminded him of his past promises. Promises that, in their view, he didn't keep. They apologized about pointing this out. He didn't think they sounded sincere. Still, for him to be angry wouldn't be strategic. So, he decided to exercise self-control, and he went very quiet so they would know they had gone too far, without him having to say anything. But maybe they were using the same strategy, because they weren't saying anything either.

So, things went quiet on the phone. Then someone coughed and someone else, it might have been Alan or Roger, said they would *have to* take possession. *Must*, like it was a law or something, or ordained by God. At five. Just like that. Like Marlon hadn't just phoned. Suddenly, Marlon was very frightened. He forgot the game plan and he begged. They tried to stop him. They sounded embarrassed. He kept begging. He pleaded. He got emotional. He sounded frightened. Desperate. His voice was cracking a little. He begged some more.

They went all quiet, like before, so maybe they had been taught to do this. To avoid people telling them their backstory and then getting them to make a decision that wouldn't be profitable. Marlon thought he heard them whispering to each other. Then they repeated, in a normal speaking voice, "Sorry, but this has gone on long enough. Sorry. Really. Sorry. But at five," Roger said, "it's done."

Marlon stood and screamed. No one could hear, as there were eighteen-inch thick walls. But Alan and Roger, they heard him. This was probably something they were used to. They probably went on a mortgage company corporate retreat, to learn how to deal with people who screamed when they were losing their homes. They hung up. Poof.

So, that was it. Marlon had burnt a bridge. He had stirred the pot. He had not been strategic. Now he had to do something else.

37. HITTING A BRIDGE SUPPORT AT A HUNDRED AND FIVE MPH

Once I had saved up my money, I was going to buy the helicopter and surprise Mr. Liebowitz, who thought I was just 'a damned kid' who didn't buy stuff. Actually I was someone to be reckoned with.

Also, I had lost my parents, mainly to do with them driving too fast in a car because it was exciting for them to think they might die, right up until the time they did.

I had suffered more than other people and I didn't get as big an allowance as other kids, I should mention. So, as you can see, my life wasn't all roses.

Have you considered, maybe I was *entitled* to the Remco Whirlybird US Airforce Rescue Corps helicopter, because I had suffered? I am not sure someone can be called bad if they have suffered. For example, I think thieves should get a free pass if their parents hit a bridge support at a hundred and five miles per hour. They couldn't even find all the parts of my mother's body.

It was kind of exciting as I left the store with a plastic toy helicopter propeller in my pocket.

Clickity chickity chickity chickity.

38. A GIFT

This was the beginning of my life of crime, but it really was just a temporary life of crime, because a real thief never intends to buy the things they steal.

Later, I went to the store to the Remco helicopter box and took the little doors and the wheel assembly, and then the left fuselage and the right fuselage, and the flight cabin. A little each time. I also took the decals you put on the outside of the fuselage, so it would look like a real Airforce helicopter. The glue to put it all together was in aisle three and that was harder to get without being seen, but I got that too.

One day, I was surprised when I moved the Scotch tape and opened the box and looked inside and there was nothing left but the directions.

At home that night and the next night, I put it all together. I hadn't done much modelling before, and those experts in the store would have done a much better job. For example, I got glue on my fingers and touched everything, so there were gluey finger marks all over the fuselage. I got glue on the little plastic windows and couldn't get it off and then the windows were all smeary and messy. I bought some paint from Mr. Liebowitz, who seemed pleased that I finally bought something. He turned out to be nice and gave me advice and he became kind of a mentor to me. He asked me what model I was painting and how come I didn't buy it from him as he considered me a loyal customer. He said in the future he would be sure and give me a big discount on anything I bought. He said that also, as he knew my aunt, ("poor woman," he said, for some reason) and she was always kind to him, that he would give me an even bigger discount in the future.

It seemed my aunt was trying to help him locate his sister, who had been in one of the camps, not camp *Wild Pony*, but one of those ones in Poland. I heard my aunt say to a friend once that there was no hope, but she couldn't tell the *old man* because hope sustained him. I realized later that Mr. Liebowitz and the old man were the same person. He didn't seem a very hopeful person, but that's just me.

I never brought the model back into the store, because he would have figured out how I got it. Using an old model of his, he showed me how to paint and take glue off windows and make a model look like the real thing on the box. He said I had a good head on my shoulders and would go far. He could tell, as he knew a thing or two about business. And when his sister joined him, maybe they would hire me, as he had plans to expand.

I got to helping close the store at night as he was getting old, and I suspected he would die soon. I didn't ask for pay or anything, as in my head I knew I still kinda owed him for the Remco Whirlybird US Airforce Rescue Corps helicopter, so I figured my work was like an interest payment against the debt. I was learning about business stuff like interest payments.

He used to show me other models I might be interested in, or maybe he thought I might buy one eventually. But I didn't, as I had learned the value of a dollar, and as he said, I had a good head on my shoulders.

Then one Christmas, when he was talking to the old model makers about different models, he called me over and reached behind the counter and handed me a bag with a ribbon on it.

I could tell there was a model inside. Maybe he thought I was poor, because I didn't spend my allowance, and my aunt was thought strange ("poor woman"). Mr. Liebowitz said, "With all your paints and brushes, you need a big model to practice your skills. Something to work on. Your chef-d'œuvre," (my aunt would like that). He told me to open it when I got home. I went home, and I reached in the bag, and it was The Remco Whirlybird US Airforce Rescue Corps helicopter.

But it was just the empty box.

39. WIGGLE ROOM

Marlon wasn't panicked. His heart was racing a little. He would jump from idea to idea in his head. Different ideas. *Boom.* Solutions. Something. He would figure it out. He would figure it out.

Then something happened. Everything was shaking and falling. The sound was like a high-speed massive old freight train; right next to you, running you over. One of those swimming, liquid-type earthquakes. The vintage canned goods were jumping off the shelf and landing on the cement floor. Marlon lived in Southern California, and this happened sometimes. To be accurate, it might have been a foreshock or an aftershock. It gets nuanced. Anyway, the earth shook. It wasn't the end of the world. It was really small when you compare it to, say, a nuclear explosion, with its Gamma rays and fallout. But it was also big. Bridges were breaking, roads cracking, some older buildings collapsing.

Marlon could see things swaying on his security cameras. The thing about an earthquake is you don't know if it's going to get worse or better, or when it's going to stop. *Which is exactly like with bad things that happen in life*, Marlon thought. *Thinking of an earthquake as a metaphor shows a presence of mind*, he also thought. He thought he smelled gas. He wondered what that was from.

One of his TVs was on a local news station, and they mentioned the quake. Sometimes you just want your experiences validated by someone saying what you just experienced, because they also experienced it. The news channel said the quake had really happened. And it was pretty big.

Marlon couldn't see that the metal beams that supported the concrete slab above him had all cracked. He also couldn't see the gas pipe that ran through the wall had a small crack in it. A crack that was getting worse with each shake.

Marlon checked on Viola via WhatsApp. She was okay. She wanted him to come up from the fallout shelter. But she didn't say it in a friendly way. He couldn't. Not yet. He still had two hundred and thirteen thousand, eight hundred dollars and forty-two cents to get. He couldn't stop. He had to act. He made more calls. The bank. Nope. Some friends. He tried a few times. They wouldn't pick up. He left messages.

Marlon was putting himself on lots of hooks. No grey area. No wiggle-room. He was a person who lived in the wiggle room. He needed wiggle room.

After all the calls, he re-examined his options. He regrouped. He told himself, "You aren't done yet, not by a long shot." He rang the mortgage company again. He tried a different method. He tried to sound like an old friend. Like they shared some special understanding about how the world works, between them. "We get it, right?" "We have been around the block." "This isn't our first rodeo." They told him to stop calling. The giant clock showed ten-thirty.

40. A GOOD BOY

After I got the Christmas present empty Remco helicopter box from Mr. Liebowitz, I felt bad. If you feel bad about something, it means that you have a moral anchor. Sociopaths steal things and don't feel bad. That's because they are sociopaths. I would feel bad about stealing things and so I knew I wasn't a sociopath.

I was going to go back and see Mr. Liebowitz, but I didn't, because the whole helicopter empty box thing became an elephant in the room between us.

Mr. Liebowitz died two years later.

My aunt said to me that it was sad because he never found out what happened to his sister. I think Mr. Liebowitz had a pretty good idea of what happened to his sister, but that's the sort of elephant in the room you just leave there.

My aunt also said that she saw Mr. Liebowitz just before he died, and he said that she should send his regards to me and that I was a good boy. She gave me a big smile because that was the sort of report she liked to get.

She said he also asked if I had finished making the model helicopter. She said she told him she thought I had, because it was hanging in my room from a wire. I wished she hadn't told him that.

41. TU VAS BIEN?

My aunt had lots of little things around the house. She covered every surface with little chachkas. My aunt went to France a couple of times. My aunt wanted to say to the world (le monde) that she was French. Which she wasn't. Some people think that by buying things, you can purchase an identity. That may be true.

I do know we aren't what we seem to be. For example, people think I am a cryptocurrency salesman. But I'm a cryptocurrency salesman who has a great collection of French literature. And, by the way, I also have thirty-three different models of the Eiffel Tower in different materials, including brass, aluminum, glass, and stone. That's a little nuance you may not expect in a cryptocurrency salesman. So, I am more than a crypto salesman. I have interests and maybe guilt. That means I have moral anchor. *Ne me jugez pas. J'ai un ancrage moral. Donc je ne suis pas un sociopathe.*

My aunt would talk about her time in France a lot. When she was young. People like to talk about how crazy/eccentric they were when they were young, even if they weren't crazy/eccentric, so the fact they have settled into a conventional life seems more like a result rather than a surrender.

I'm not sure if my aunt was trying to say that she was crazy or eccentric when she was young. I think she just really liked the idea of Franceness. She didn't like the idea of being a *spinster* living in the Midwest. Our pastor called her a spinster like it was a good thing. She said something to him under her breath and she never went to church again. She wasn't really a spinster anyway. She was single all her life, because the French guy that she met in France didn't come to see her, even though he promised he would. That's different from a spinster. The rest of her life she was mourning for him or maybe for France, or maybe for not having ever been crazy or eccentric.

Maybe that was her elephant in the room. The ordinariness with which she didn't want to be associated. Being French wasn't ordinary. Except in France. But she wasn't in France. She was in the American Midwest.

In an effort to be clear that she wasn't ordinary, she had:

1. Many French chachkas.
2. Thirty-three Eiffel towers of different sizes and materials.
3. A baguette made from pottery.
4. Fifty-three French books (François Sagan, Saint-Exupéry, Malraux, Hergé etc.)
5. Six posters from the Maîtres de l'Affiche.
6. Nine reproductions of paintings by Cézanne.
7. Four French cookbooks.
8. An old-fashioned French-looking bicycle which had a wicker basket.
9. Three berets in different colors.
10. One French language course on CD, called Instant Travel French for Lovers.
11. Two French phrase books.
12. One damaged Chanel clutch bag.
13. Six maps of Paris.
14. One framed photo of Catherine Deneuve.
15. One small bottle of Chanel Number Five.

French language peppered her conversation when we went out together. She said we were going out, *ensemble*. When she felt something was standard, she would say, *de rigueur*. When she hoped for something, and she hoped for lots of things, she would say, *J'espère*. She called our pastor *une crotte du chèvre*.

I was accused once of cheating in school, which I said was entirely untrue, but of course was entirely true. My aunt believed me, though she did ask about the model helicopter from Mr. Liebowitz's store. The fact I might have stolen the model was beyond her moral comprehension. Just like she believed the promise from the French guy.

Some people are just easy to fool.

But things were starting to add up even to her. Fortunately, a distraction intervened before her doubt became a crisis. It was parents' night at my school, and she went and met most of my teachers, including my French teacher. They spoke French together. I was proud of my aunt because although she spoke slowly, my French teacher smiled and responded. My French teacher generally had a frown as to imply that everybody was a little bit stupid, which seemed painful to her. But my aunt and her spoke for like ten or fifteen sentences. In French. My aunt was on cloud nine.

After that, at worst, she thought maybe her nephew (me) might have stolen something and maybe he cheated on an exam. But her nephew would be okay. He would find his way and be a good person. And maybe the French guy would come to visit her after all. It was possible. My aunt was on kind of a French language high after speaking to my French teacher and also, she was delusional her entire life.

42. A BIG-ASSED GUN

Marlon opened his desk drawer and took out a big-assed handgun. A Desi. The 50 Calibre Desert Eagle. He loaded it with real bullets. Marlon started pretending he was a secret agent, or a Black-Ops guy on a mission. Crouching, pivoting, spinning, pointing the gun, imagining firing, then spinning again.

He put the gun back in the drawer. Still loaded. Still cocked. The clock showed eleven o'clock. The time was moving fast. He shouldn't have been playing. He went to an online pawnbroker site, *EASY CASH AND PAWN*. They connected via Google Hang-Out. They knew each other. Not the first call.

He showed them his Rolex. The old pawnbrokers said he had to come in. They always said that. They should trust him by now. He asked for just an estimate. They didn't want to give it to him. But he was really turning on the charm, so they said, "Okay, let's have a look."

He held the Rolex up close to the computer's camera. The two pawnbrokers looked at each other. They tried not to smile. They had to try to not smile a lot in their profession. People are easily humiliated when they are desperate for money. Smiling then is a bad thing. But sometimes it's best just to say what you are thinking. Besides, Marlon was a borderline crank. So, they told him, *it was a fake*.

This really made Marlon mad. He told them he would be taking his business elsewhere in the future. He told them he just completed a stock market trade and made a load of money. So, their loss. This made them smile. They tried not to, but they were smiling when he disconnected from Google Hang-Out.

The big clock showed eleven-fifteen. How could that have taken fifteen minutes? Marlon had read lots of self-help books.

One said:

1. The trick is to keep going.
5. The trick is to get up when you get knocked down.
6. The trick is seeing each failure as a necessary step to success.
9. The trick is believing, even when no one else does.
10. The trick is to put one foot in front of another. The trick is keeping momentum.
11. The trick is not stopping.

The book may have been called *The Trick is… 25 Tricks to Become Truly Successful*, but he wasn't sure. Its main recurring theme was that you shouldn't give up. He couldn't remember nineteen of the twenty-five tricks. But they were all pretty much the same thing. Don't give up. And he wasn't going to. He strategized. He regrouped. He called the mortgage company again. This time the receptionist wouldn't put his call through. The receptionist. Marlon was trying to be nice to the receptionist, because she was probably a very junior person and didn't understand the way the world worked. But she was not behaving in a respectful fashion. A receptionist at a mortgage company should behave in a respectful fashion, talking to people who need money. It is a sensitive topic. She was making a typical junior person mistake. Because she worked for a company, didn't mean she WAS the company. She was just a junior person. She probably couldn't even afford a mortgage of her own. Even if they gave her a special deal as a junior person in the company. So, who was she really when all was said and done? But she didn't seem to understand this. She was behaving like she was a REAL mortgage person. So, Marlon spoke to her in a very firm way. He reminded her that she was a receptionist, and he was a client of the company, and she should think about that and what if, for example, he had just made a lot of money on the stock market? Then she would have offended a very wealthy client, and that would be a whole different thing, wouldn't it? And she said,

"Did you?" And Marlon said, "Did I what?" And she said, "Make a lot of money on the stock market?" It sounded sarcastic. So, Marlon put the phone down, because you can't fix stupid.

He took out the Desert Eagle gun again, it was still cocked, which by the way, you shouldn't do with a Desert Eagle unless you are about to shoot it. Then Marlon moved into a low crouch. He imagined he arrived at the mortgage company, just as some terrorist had taken all the mortgage company staff hostage, because maybe the terrorist was behind on his mortgage, which shows it can happen to anyone.

The terrorist had Alan and Roger and the receptionist tied up. And it looked like he was going to do something bad. And even though the mortgage company had treated Marlon terribly, Marlon did a series of forward rolls, into the mortgage office, to confuse the terrorist, then he jumped and shot the terrorist and saved Alan and Roger and the receptionist, and they all said *thank-you*. It was only when he took off his Black-Ops balaclava that they recognized who he was and then they said *sorry* about the mortgage thing, and *listen, don't worry about it now. The house is yours.* He put the gun back in the drawer. Still loaded, still cocked and ready.

43. I LOVE YOU

As I reached adolescence, my aunt began to annoy me. She said she loved me all the time and she waited for me to respond. It was gross. Just because you say something, doesn't mean you mean it.

The expression *I love you* has a short shelf life.

No one thinks about it; they say it willy-nilly because they must in certain circumstances, and if you don't, it's a *big deal*.

I suspect that even partners who are really in love get tired of having to say it. And then tired of feeling it. It's hard to be in love all the time. In fact, I bet that when we wake up in the morning, we scan our lives for things we find annoying, not scan the room for things we love. They are just there. Probably saying, annoyingly, they love us. I mean, fuck.

When I was thirteen, I said to my aunt, "You're not French. Why do you pretend to be French?" She suddenly looked very old and sad. She said she *wasn't pretending to be French,* she just *enjoyed French culture*, and I said that *French culture was stupid* and she said, "You don't know much about it then," and then we had an argument. We didn't mention it again. Because.

Later, she began hiding some of her French things and was a little bit less French.

She didn't wear her red beret, which she loved, at the next parent-teachers' night. She spoke to the French teacher. In English.

44. THE CAT BURGLAR

My aunt had a collection of jewelry. By this time, I knew the value of a dollar. I had read magazines about people finding treasures right at home. A painting that was in an attic that was bought for five dollars at a flea market, turned out to be a Cézanne. Cézanne's *La Montagne Saint-Victoire* sold for a hundred and thirty-seven million dollars. *Par exemple.*

I saw a movie with Cary Grant and Grace Kelly, and he was a much-admired cat burglar in the South of France. *To Catch a Thief*, it was called. I recommend it. People often admire criminals if they show ingenuity, are good-looking and don't hurt anyone. I think this goes back to the idea all property is theft. We don't admire property, but we admire good looks. Cary Grant was innocent, in the end, anyway. He had real moral anchor, even though HE USED to be a cat burglar. People change. So, we should forgive them for the things they did before they changed. Because now they have moral anchor.

My aunt said we must deal with the consequences of our actions. That goes with the moral anchor thing. But doesn't go so well with our entitlement (because we have suffered) thing. Also, the excitement thing (as we leave toy stores with a propeller in our pocket, or my parents driving too fast and dying when I needed them).

I wondered if my aunt's jewelry box was actually full of treasures, and she didn't even know it. She almost never went out. I mean socially. She might buy a frozen baguette, or see my teacher about my so-called cheating, but that was it. Obviously, the French guy wasn't going to visit, so the jewelry was a waste. All she could do was LOOK at her jewelry. But the jewelry was important to her. She was the same with the chachkas. I said we *didn't need thirty-three Eiffel Towers,* and that made her cry. So, I let it go before it became an argument. But seriously, *thirty-three* Eiffel Towers?

I thought that if there were treasures in her jewelry box, we should sell them and get some serious money. Then she could buy a ticket to France and track that French guy down and go right to his house and say, *Bonjour. Come on, what's up with you? I have been waiting vingt-cinq years.* I also thought that if we sold her jewelry, I could also buy myself a few things and I wouldn't have to be on an allowance, I could invest it, for example. But she wasn't going to sell the jewelry. This was obvious. She wasn't going to see the wood through the trees. Something had to be done, and I admit that I was excited when I decided to steal the bracelet that the French guy had given her. It was exciting, because I might get caught. And I was excited because I knew that I was doing the right thing.

I heard about something called a pawn shop. There's someone there called a pawnbroker. They take your things, and they give you money for them. What's cool is you can come back later and get your things back. If you remember. Or can. So, the plan was that I would 'pawn' her bracelet, get a lot of money, maybe invest it, then buy her a house or a watch, or a car or maybe more jewelry. The house would take a while. I would have to pawn other things. And invest.

On the day of the theft, I was nervous. My aunt called out to me as she was leaving and she said, "I'm leaving, I love you," and I yelled back, "I love you too." She went off on her French-looking, old-fashioned bicycle.

I went into her bedroom and looked around and read some love letters she had written, I guess to the French guy, as they were partially written in French. They were kinda soppy and pathetic. Lots of *Je t'aime, Je t'aime, encore et encore et blah et blah et blah.* They also made me a little angry on behalf of my aunt. She was a good person. He should have treated her better.

I knew she'd be out shopping for a while. I opened the jewelry box and looked at her treasures. I made pirate sounds as I did so.

Aargg. Booty, I said in a pirate-type voice.

I put on some clip-on earrings. I put on the bracelet the French guy (who wasn't getting unsent love letters) gave her. In the mirror, I looked like a pirate who was thirteen. Who doesn't like pirates? Lovable sea-faring cat burglars. Good-looking, in a rugged pirate sort of way. I was having fun before I made my getaway. Also, I was nervous.

Aargg, I said again. I wondered what my aunt would do when she found the bracelet missing. Poor woman, as Mr. Liebowitz would say. Then...

    1. I heard her door key in the front door. She must have forgotten something. *Aargg.*

    2. I froze. *Aargg.*

    3. I heard her coming up the stairs. *Aargg.*

    4. She called my name. *Aargg.*

    5. I didn't move.

    6. She was at the end of the hall. I still didn't move.

    7. I was going to be caught. She was going to know that all her suspicions about the exam and about the model helicopter and me lacking moral anchor had been right. She was walking down the hall.

    8. Then I moved.

    9. I quickly put the earrings back in the jewelry box.

    10. She was right outside the door.

    11. I tried to put the bracelet back, and it wouldn't fit in the box. I opened the lid again and tried to jam it in. It wouldn't jam. I stuffed it in my pocket. I thought I did. But it was only half in. It was dangling out.

    12. She was opening the door.

    13. I jumped under her bed.

She came into the room.

The bed was high. I was easy to see. But she hadn't, yet. She moved around the room. She got some things. She put a jacket on. She started singing a song by Édith Piaf. She called my name again. She went out the door to look for me. This was my chance. I ran across the hall and into the bathroom, inches behind her. I could have touched her. The bracelet fell out of my pocket. I just caught it. Once in the bathroom, I turned the water on. And she came back and knocked on the door and said, "Are you in there?" And I said "What?" like I couldn't hear her, and then she said again, "Are you in there?" And I said, "Yeah, I'm in here." She said she forgot something and then she said, a *bientot* and she was gone, stopping only to yell, "I love you," still humming the Piaf song, *Non, Je Ne Regrette Rien*. But of course, she did. Regret, I mean. The song says the singer regrets nothing. But my aunt regretted everything. Probably including her having to raise me. Though she never said it. Instead, she said *I love you* to me all the time. It was as annoying as fuck. And sad.

Meanwhile, I had crossed the Rubicon. I put the bracelet in my pocket and got on my own bicycle and headed for the pawn broker. My heart was still beating from nearly getting caught. It was awful. But it was exciting. My poor aunt, but most of all, poor me. I had suffered, after all.

45. A GOSSAMER THREAD

Viola was thinking about the upcoming phone call. Phone calls are dangerous. Leaving messages is dangerous. Evidence of what a bad mother you are. In her son's sixteen-year-old view.

She loved her son. But he was complex. She was allowed to say complex. She wasn't allowed to say *angry* or *volatile* or *depressed*. That would upset him. And he was delicate. She wasn't allowed to say *delicate* either. Most of all. It is easier to make small children happy. Sometimes you just must kiss a bruised knee. When they are older it is more complex. All that time he spent in his room. Staring at the ceiling. Playing those video games. Once, upset about some girl. Saying little. Maybe it was all their fault. They were his parents. His sister wasn't like that. But she wasn't allowed to mention his sister either. Particularly to praise her. That would be bad.

When did he start to change?

He'd once said he was going to be a writer. Well, actually, Viola had said it. She said, "Someday, you are going to be a writer, I sense it." And he had said, "Maybe." Shortly after that, it went all blurry in her mind. He got very bad, so they put him on medication. Olanzapine, then some others. But he stopped taking them, apparently. Something happened. She tried to remember what it was. She couldn't.

Then, somehow, she was on medication for some reason. She couldn't remember why that happened either. But she knew she had to be careful on her calls to him, because he was delicate. But she wanted him to know that she was there for him. When he emerged from wherever he was. Sometimes she would wake in the daytime, and it was odd because she couldn't remember sleeping. The dreams seemed to be a different type of wakefulness. And she would wake at night, as if in a different dream. It made telling time hard. Or having a sense of time or its passage, hard. This made her even more cautious. She realized she might misspeak, as she was so uncertain about so many things. Everything really. She might say the wrong thing and he would never come back. She was failing him. She knew this. He was in such profound pain but would grow terribly angry if she mentioned therapy.

"You are humiliating me," he would say to her. She didn't want him to feel humiliated. But she knew somehow how important her calls to him were. It was the delicate, gossamer thread that linked him to the world. She held the other end of the thread. It was frightening to her. One time she got it wrong. It had all become too much and she had screamed at him on the phone.

Saying nothing really, just screaming, until finally, quietly saying:

Come home.

But he didn't. And he didn't say anything either. He never did.

46. CONSEQUENCES

The pawnbroker didn't like me. I wanted him to like me.

He looked at the bracelet through a little spyglass. He asked me where I got it. I said that my aunt had left it to me. She was run over by a truck in France. It was a Renault truck.

He didn't care how my aunt died.

He seemed okay with the 'piece'. He said he would give me a thousand dollars for it. I was thinking five thousand, but I didn't say that because if I was wrong, it would reveal I didn't know much about jewelry.

My aunt would be pleased, once she got over the whole I stole from her thing. Maybe she didn't know about pawn shops. A thousand dollars was a lot of money. Then I got concerned and decided to delay telling my aunt about pawning her bracelet. I would wait until she was in a really good mood or maybe was thinking she needed money.

I went behind Kelly's Dry Cleaning and took the money out of the envelope the pawnbroker had given me. I had never seen that much money before. It was more than all the money I had saved up from my allowance.

Then I thought about consequences. My aunt said everybody in life either thinks about consequences after they do something, or before they do something. Her view was that it is better to think about consequences before you do something. I get that, but then you might not do anything ever. So, my view became to do stuff without thinking and deal with the consequences later. *Aargg.* This way I could be assured of doing lots of interesting things and not ending up like my aunt.

Still, as regards the bracelet, I decided to have a good think about it.

Later that night I could hear my aunt moving around in her bedroom.

Then opening and closing doors all around the house.

And then moving the furniture.

And then crying.

I heard her ringing the police and saying that she thought there might have been a break-in. But the police couldn't understand why a burglar would only take one piece. She must have lost it last time she wore it out. She finished the call to the police and began to cry again.

Then she came into my room and asked if I was okay. She was sorry to wake me, but she said that someone had stolen her very precious bracelet, which was worth thousands and thousands of dollars. *What?* I wanted to shout, *the pawnbroker ripped us off*, because it was her money too, but I didn't.

To be helpful in her investigation, I asked detective-type questions. *When had she last seen it? Were there any signs of a break-in? Are you sure it is really worth that much?*

We went outside in the middle of the night and looked for clues. I went to a back window and stamped around. Then I said to my aunt, look at these *footprints* over here. She looked at my footprints and said those footprints looked fresh and weren't they just mine?

Then we went inside, and we sat on the sofa, and she looked at me with an expression that said, *Is there something you want to tell me?* But she didn't say it out loud. I hate when people have that expression on their face because:

1. You can't respond.
2. You can't spin a web of deceit.
3. You can't bullshit.
4. You can't dissemble.
5. You can't lie.
6. You can't create a narrative.

7. You can't tell a tale.
8. You can't undo their thinking.

All because they won't tell you what they're thinking. They don't accuse you in a proper way, so that you can deny everything.

My aunt looked at me right in the eyes. As if she was almost giving up on me. Saying with her sad look, that I had to decide the difference between right and wrong. I guess she didn't really know me very well.

Because I didn't say anything at all.

47. THE BIG SECRET

Things got so bad with the repossession and the money and everything for Marlon, that he finally phoned me. What took him so long? Me, the maker of dreams. But some things I am not. I am not a charity. I am not a mental health professional. I am not a marriage counselor. I am not a lender of money.

Marlon tells me his sad backstory. I know why. He wants to make himself human. He wants me to lend him money. I am not lending him money. So, I said, "Maybe, let me think about it. What about collateral?" This was strategic. What was he going to do? Offer me his soon-to-be-repossessed house? He probably would have. He's the kind of guy to do that. He would say, "You can have my house as security. Just don't tell Viola."

I didn't let him say it. Time is money. Here is some information for nothing: when people talk to you, they are stealing your money from you. Every minute speaking to a loser is a minute you could be using to make money. And if you aren't making money, you are losing money.

I looked at the clock. Marlon was still talking: short-term cash flow, blah, blah; his wife, blah, blah; the bad advice I gave him on his last investment, blah, blah; his son, blah, blah, blah.

I should have hung up. But I am a philosopher. And maybe also because of my aunt, who encouraged me to think about things differently. That's why I am a philosopher of sorts. People with a lot of life experience become philosophers.

For example, here is one thing I say that is philosophical: *if you give a man a fish, he starves in a month.* Depending on the size of the fish. *Give him a line and a hook, and he will never be hungry.*

I had the solution Marlon needed. The most incredible of solutions. A solution that would change his life forever. I would give him a fishing line and the ultimate, nuclear-powered hook.

Crypto currency. The mother-fucking future, motherfuckers.

I sent him a video. It was called, *Get Rich Quick. GRQ.* It was slickly made with cool graphics. It was all about a financial instrument that would provide the opportunity to make a lot of money in a hurry, but only for a select few. Fortunately for Marlon, I was in a position to let Marlon in. Because I liked him. And after that terrible thing that happened to him and his wife, you had to feel something for the guy, even when he was lying to your face.

I told him the minimum play was 50K. I couldn't mess around, so I said, "Do you have it?" He laughed. He asked if I was *fucking kidding*? He said he had way more than that. *Way more.*

This contradicted his earlier sob story. God, he was shameless. But my aunt often said, *Good manners are pretending you don't notice things.*

Like when I stole that bracelet that the man who didn't come back had given her. And she said, "Have you seen it?"

And I said, "No, I haven't."

And she said, "It was the only thing I had left to remember him."

As if that would make it, or him, come back.

48. A PERSON CAN DO BAD THINGS

I was angry with my aunt after the whole mystery surrounding the disappearing bracelet thing. I was thinking about it, and she said the bracelet was really valuable. But the pawn broker at Easy Cash and Pawn, a licensed professional and a subject matter expert, said it was only worth a thousand dollars *at the most*. So, she was lying, just like everyone. Nobody is innocent, so please.

That night, after the whole mysterious disappearance, my aunt smoked more Gauloises than usual and looked sadder than usual. At bedtime, I waited for her to come up and try to teach me something about physics or something, but she didn't. So, I just stared at the ceiling above my bed, wondering how many Sieverts I was absorbing.

Over the next few days, she worked for a long time on making a card. It was white and square, and the size of a greeting card. Like for a birthday. She decorated it with tiny flowers, and birds and fish. She was pretty good at drawing. One night she gave me the card, slowly, like it was something valuable, or secret. On one side of the card, she had written: *The statement on the other side of this card is untrue.* So, I flipped the card over and on the other side she had written: *The statement on the other side of this card is true.*

When I looked up, she had moved really close to me and was right up in my face, I mean, I was looking right at that overlapping tooth. With a little bit of Gauloises tobacco stuck in it. And she said, "A person can do a bad thing and be a good person. We shouldn't judge. They may have their good reasons for the bad things." She was staring at me, really close.

I guess the subject being discussed was the mysteriously missing bracelet that the man who wasn't coming back had given her. Maybe it was about other things as well. Physics and paradoxes, and wanting more than you can have, and ignoring things to be courteous and a lot of other things too, that I was too tired to think about.

I looked back at her and said, "I don't know who took it. I wish I did, because I know how important it is to you."

49. MAKING A MOVIE

I told Marlon that if he put that money up before one o'clock, he would earn five hundred thousand by five. A once in a lifetime offer. I said my fiduciary responsibility as a financial counselor forbade me from making a guarantee, but he should read between the lines. So, I didn't actually make a guarantee.

That said, I told him that I was going to take a considerable risk and tell him something I shouldn't. Because I liked him. But I swore him to secrecy. No one could know.

He said, *okay.*

People love being in the know, particularly when it is secret. It makes them feel special. That's why if you want to get people to believe something, whisper. This is called a *sales technique*. And as everyone is selling all the time, sales techniques are important skills to learn. I was on a Zoom call with Marlon. I leaned forward into the screen, and whispered, that *at one o'clock* there was *going to be an announcement* that would *rock the crypto market*. "Some Hollywood people," I said very quietly, "are going to announce they are doing a film called GRQ." Then I leaned back and looked around his fallout shelter to make sure no one was listening. It looked like the coast was clear, so I went on: "It's going to be a real movie. You know, a feature film, widely released and then on Netflix or one of those. Think about it dude, a movie about crypto. I mean if Elon Musk can make a joke and move the market, what will a film do?" I hate when people interrupt me mid-pitch. But Marlon did.

"What's it about?" he asked.

I wanted to say, who cares? "You mean the story? Seriously? It's about crypto, that's what will move the market. The story? Okay. It's actually about some fucking guy investing in a crypto coin called GRQ. The guy is a loser, a failure, and a liar. He gets into trouble. You know, the audience will wonder, how will he get out of this situation? That's what will make the drama. Or the comedy. Or the tragedy. Or whatever it is. But seriously, dude, why does it matter?"

Marlon asked, "What if it isn't good?"

I sighed deeply, thinking you can't save people from themselves. That isn't your job. But I said something different. I said, "Maybe the film will suck. It doesn't matter. But what does matter in the crypto world is it is a big publicity event. A big publicity event will drive the price. And even if it doesn't, everyone will think it will, so that will drive the price. And even the announcement of the film will drive the price and later, when the film comes out (and even if the film sucks), that will drive the price. It's a paradox. Crypto doesn't rely on anything except perception. And when its price goes up, that will drive the price."

Marlon said, "I still don't get it." Not the quickest bunny in the forest.

"It's simple. You don't have to worry about determining the value of it, because it's not based on anything. It's like the lottery. But with better odds. So, it isn't based on something someone makes, or invents, or manufactures, or creates. It isn't impacted by the underlying value of some company's profit and loss and inventory and all that nonsense. Nope. Just perception, publicity, and rumors."

The light went on in his head. He understood. So, there it was. I had presented Marlon with this opportunity. Sometimes, the words just flow. I could rest.

Marlon said, "I'm not that interested."

I'm throwing this guy a life preserver, and he isn't interested? You will be thinking, surely you told him to fuck off? I didn't. Because I am a nice person. Despite what you think.

50. THE QUALITY OF MERCY

My aunt, who is appearing in this story more than I had intended, would say, *the quality of mercy is not strained. It droppeth as the gentle rain from heaven.*

I am not a merciful person. Merciful persons fall for a backstory. Suckers. I am not a sucker. My aunt was merciful. But it didn't help her much, did it? Look what happened to her bracelet.

As for Marlon, I could smell his desperation. And desperation provides opportunities. Not for the desperate. Still, he threw the opportunity right in my face. Nobody says thank you.

I said, "Okay, good luck." And I hung up. Another good sales technique is to make people fearful of missing out. Sure enough. *Boom.* Marlon panicked. I was his lifeboat, and he just jumped off the lifeboat. He wasn't sure whether he was right or wrong. He was panicking.

For the next thirty minutes, Marlon was all over the internet. Looking up everything to do with crypto. Boom. And GRQ. Boom. He read articles about crypto. Boom. Videos about crypto. Boom, boom. News stories about crypto. Boom. One after the other: crypto graphs, crypto prognostications, crypto experts talking on finance shows about crypto. Boom, boom, boom, boom. All the crypto things he could find. A crypto research frenzy.

He had the crypto stories playing on his big screen television in his fallout shelter/office/man cave. He had them playing at the same time on his multiple computer screens. It was a crypto fest. He was in a crypto passion. He was crypto-obsessed. And best of all, crypto-needy. Financial opportunity is a high-speed train that only stops briefly at your station, or so you at that moment believe.

This was a problem for Marlon. He had non-buyer's remorse. And he wanted to fix that, but he had another problem. He didn't have the minimum investment I told him he needed. Marlon knew now there was a way out. I was it. GRQ was it. He could save his house. His marriage. Everything. But he needed fifty thousand dollars.

My aunt used to say, *if you do the same thing twice and expect a different result, then you are crazy.* She did the same thing every day, and didn't get a different result, but I suspect she had given up on results.

Marlon would have to go back to his friends. All those who had told him to fuck off. But Marlon figured he had an ace up his sleeve. This time he wasn't asking them to lend him money. This time they were INVESTING. He was doing them a favor. This was a game changer.

He began working the phones. Some friends hung up. Others would try to avoid the topic and then hang up or be called away to something important. Marlon didn't believe all the excuses.

Some other friends gave him the talk, starting with, *Can I speak truthfully?* Marlon knew already that if anyone ever starts a sentence like that, you should always answer, *No, you can't.* But Marlon forgot to say no you can't and they said something like: *You lie.* And Marlon responded with something like: *Well, you think you are so superior and you're not,* and it went downhill from there.

People get funny when talking about money. It brings out the worst in them. Marlon thought this too. He noted that several friends made a point of remembering that he hadn't paid back some small sum in the past.

After a lot of calls, not a single so-called friend had invested any money with Marlon. Noted, Marlon thought. I won't forget. Wow. If it was the other way around, I would have been there for them.

51. FAMILY

So, Marlon went to option B.

The thing about family is family is different. They won't let you miss an opportunity, the way friends will. Families will ignore the bad things you do. They won't put the phone down on you.

When Marlon phoned his mother, she didn't hang up on him. She listened to the whole pitch. She was interested, though at first, she thought crypto was that thing where they freeze you, so when medical science improves, you can be brought back to life. Marlon explained it wasn't that.

He said, "Mom, I know I'm a failure, I know no one loves me." She told him that was *silly nonsense*. His daughter loved him, Viola loved him. She loved him. And she was going to invest with him because she really believed in him absolutely. Then she offered him a thousand dollars. She said, "I can give you a thousand dollars." That was painful for her. She was worried about how long her savings were going to last. But Marlon was her only child.

Then Marlon said, "The minimum I can accept is ten thousand dollars." Marlon was aware of how late it was, and he had to dispense with niceties. She said, "That's all my savings. It's all I have in the world."

Marlon said he wouldn't risk her money unless it was a sure thing. He wanted her to finally live in luxury. That's what he had always wanted for her. She heard the desperation in his voice. She took a deep breath and said, "Okay, I will send you the money."

And he said, "How much money?"

And she said, "Ten thousand dollars."

She wasn't sophisticated about the internet, so he had to talk her through accessing her bank account and moving the money to his. Marlon noticed she was sad. So, he said, "My investment counselor said the minimum return on this, even if everything goes wrong, is seventy-five percent." I never said that, but Marlon figured, what were the chances I would ever meet her?

After he hung up with his mother, Marlon felt like he was on a roll. So, he reached out to his daughter, Sarah. A lot of people won't borrow from their children. After Sarah said, "How is mom?" He said, "Okay, but stressed." His daughter said, "Why?" He told her how bad things were, and that they were *going to lose everything*, and he could never, never ask her to lend him money, he was her dad, after all. But this wasn't a loan, it was an *investment opportunity*.

This made her uncomfortable but there was nothing she could do. Because he said how bad things were, so she couldn't just hang up on her father. She mentioned some of Marlon's past financial schemes that hadn't worked out. This hurt Marlon's feelings. Sarah, of all people, should have known he just had bad luck. But ever since she'd married *him*, she wasn't the same person. Marlon then talked a lot about her childhood. Then about her brother. They didn't talk about her brother much. Though they both thought about him all the time. They both cried. Marlon said, "You know, the day he died, it wasn't the way your mother tells it." And Sarah said she didn't want to talk about it and, "It doesn't matter now, Daddy, we can't un-ring a bell."

They were quiet for a long time. She was right. Bells can't be un-rung. And things can't be unseen. What he had seen that day. But that was then. He remembered another line from a self-help book: *If you can't live in the past, move on from it.*

They had talked a lot, his son Darien and him, when Darien was young. But less so when he got older. Still, he would have understood that a part of good leadership is prioritization, and right now, there was a priority. The past would always be there for Marlon to visit later. As much as you can visit the past, which isn't really much at all. You can just remember it a little. It was different for Viola. With the phone calls. But they didn't help her, and nothing about the past was going to change. It couldn't. But he couldn't go there just now. In the middle of a crisis.

So, Marlon begged his daughter. Really, hardcore, down on his knees begging. He asked her, honestly did she have money available to help her *mother* and him? He said through tears: "I hate being weak in front of you. Let me tell you, a father never wants to be weak in front of his daughter. But I don't know what to do." This seemed to work.

She told him, she and Michael (*him*, her husband) had been saving for six years. And they had twenty-five thousand dollars. They were saving up for a down-payment on an apartment for them and their new baby. "*Maybe*," she said, "we could lend you some of that?" Boom. He went really quiet. He explained again how humiliating it is for a man to ask for money from his daughter, *and now we are negotiating?* Really, he needed it all. There it is. That's it. He had never asked her for anything, and now he was. She was scared. She was worried about what Michael, her husband (*him again*) would say because *it was his money too*. And there was the baby.

That was fine. *Good for her. But he was her father before she was married. And my God, what they had all suffered. And suffering should matter, shouldn't it? Anyway, by the time Michael realized the money was out of the account, it would have tripled. And then what would he say?* Marlon said, "I bet he says, thank you." Marlon told his daughter his financial counselor had guaranteed at least a forty-five percent return, as a minimum. Actually, I never said that either.

She didn't know what to do. Marlon could see her drifting. He had to get firm. He said, "I really need you to wire me that money." Another long silence. And they were both thinking about that same thing, that same day all those years ago. So, she said she would. Send it all. But "Please, Daddy. Please don't lose it. Please." Of course, he wouldn't. He said he loved her. *I love you, little girl.* And hung up. People say *I love you* a lot.

Marlon went to the whiteboard. He added up the money from his mother and daughter. $35,000.00. Just 15K to go.

Then, his father-in-law, Charles, called him up on Skype.

Because Marlon's landline still wasn't working. Because he hadn't paid the bill. He was prioritizing. When Marlon had been first dating Viola and they were leaving The Polo Lounge after a very successful first meeting, he had heard his future father-in-law say, "This guy is a loser. Every word out of his mouth is BS. He isn't living in the *real world*." They thought he had gone to the toilet, but he was actually walking right behind them. Marlon had had the last laugh. When they had bought the house they couldn't afford and he carried her through the door, like a threshold thing, Marlon said, "I should tell your dad I am not such a loser now, am I?"

Viola wanted to encourage Marlon, so in the past, when Marlon had said, "I'm not such a loser now, am I?" she would smile in an encouraging way. But on that particular day, when Marlon carried her across the threshold, she said, "Marlon, are you sure we can afford this place?" And Marlon laughed, in a bold way, and said, "Are you joking? Now we have this place, AND I'm going to get you a new car." Years later, she looked out the window to the backyard, which was weedy. There was a cardboard box there. Some project that Marlon had abandoned. There was also that strange looking Greek model building that Marlon had planned to make into something. She couldn't remember what, but now it was broken and full of mud. And there was that fence with the barbed wire and the electric substation. From which, even from inside where she was standing, she could hear humming.

Viola was looking out the back window and could hear the humming and see the weeds, and then she remembered what the cardboard box was. Marlon had said he was going to put in a water feature, to make a nice sound. And later, a Jacuzzi. *I wonder if your dad will think I am a loser after I put in a water feature.* And the Greek building was going to go next to that, with a Greek woman statue holding a jug which would spill water into the water feature. And Viola said over the humming, though she was whispering, "I am worried about Darien." And Marlon said, and wished later he hadn't, "Don't worry about Darien. He will figure it out."

Viola looked at the ruined box. There were faded pictures of watering cans on it. When they had first moved in, Marlon had gone to Joyful Season Gardening and Lawn Care and bought a *Whimsical Floating Watering Cans Water Feature*, but he hadn't realized how many tools he would need to put all the parts together, as well as all the plumbing, and he had left it in its box outside, and it was rotting now, in a corner, next to, she remembered suddenly in her dreamy state, next to the Parthenon. Well, the model of the Parthenon. The real Parthenon wasn't in her garden. It was in Greece.

The reason Charles, his father-in-law, was reaching out now, was because Viola had phoned him and told her father about the *repossession*. She had betrayed the sacred trust between husband and wife, Marlon thought. He would forgive her; he wasn't perfect himself. He had stopped counting days for streaks to do with big deals a long time ago. They never got past a day.

His father-in-law, who had called him a loser all those years ago and never got a chance to see the water feature, now knew about the REPOSSESSION. That was even worse than the neighbors seeing the notice on the door. Marlon did feel sorry for Charles. His wife Judy, who was always quiet, like she was thinking about a lot more than she was saying, got especially quiet, and then she was diagnosed with Alzheimer's. She would still smile from time to time, like she was happier wherever she was, but no one could know for certain. Charles would sit with her for hours and hold her hand and try to reach her, but he wasn't sure what to say. He wasn't sure what to say to her even before the Alzheimer's. He sensed she was disappointed. But he had done his best. That's what he sometimes said when holding her hand. He was sorry, but he had done his best.

Marlon saw a different side of Charles. Marlon got the feeling that Charles was playing a father-in-law, like on a TV show. With his cardigan sweaters and his reading glasses and the tufts of white hair at his temples. But most of all, the TV father-in-law's judgmental looks. But there was no time for that just now. Marlon needed money and he suddenly sensed an opportunity. *You can do this,* he thought.

He told Charles: "You can't judge a man by bad luck. Only rich people want to pretend that success comes from skill and virtue, because then everyone thinks they are skillful and virtuous." Charles, his father-in-law, said, "I am not in the mood for your BS." Even though he wasn't in the mood for Marlon's BS, Marlon kept going and pitched the crypto investment to his father-in-law, the originator of the phrase, *this guy is a loser.* Marlon talked fast; he didn't want to pause. Momentum is important. Once you start something, it's easier to keep doing it. Like lying or avoiding opening the box of a water feature.

It was easiest when Marlon shut his eyes, so he couldn't see Charles, as he kept talking and kept pitching. Then it was time for the big close. The close was this: Marlon explained that he and his wife, Charles's daughter, would be on the street if Charles didn't give them money. Marlon said, "I know you don't like me, Charles. But you are our only hope."

Marlon then said, "I am a proud person, and it is hard for me to ask for help. But it really is a once-in-a-lifetime opportunity. We will be rich. Your daughter will be safe. Also, Viola mustn't know." And then Marlon said, "I know I am a loser. Pathetic. But I want to be more. I am sorry." And then he wept.

And then one of those silences again. And the old man looked sad. And spent. Not at all like a TV personality. He looked over at his silent, smiling wife and thought for a long time. And then said, Yes. To the fifteen thousand dollars.

Marlon said, "You won't regret this."

52. CLUSTER OF EARTHQUAKES

Marlon wrote $15,000.00 on the whiteboard, though he didn't have to. Because he could do the math. He had enough money. He took a moment to enjoy the sense of achievement. The sense of having really done something. *We don't spend enough time enjoying the journey*, my aunt would say. *Nous ne passons pas assez de temps à profiter de notre vie.* Though she said it in a way that made it clear she wasn't enjoying her own journey all that much.

Five minutes later, Marlon was phoning me. I ignored his call. He should have thought of this possibility when he told me he wasn't interested.

The clock was ticking. It was twelve-thirty. Thirty minutes until the press conference and the launch of the film GRQ. And the chance of a lifetime. Marlon kept phoning me. You see my thinking. The harder something is to get, the more it is valued. So, I wanted to make sure he knew I was of value. We all want other people to know we are of value, so sometimes we have to use techniques to teach them this.

But then a huge shaking *rattle, rattle, rattle. Thump, bang, crack, creak.* And a very loud RUMBLE.

Another earthquake.

A foreshock, really. Bigger. A noise like a freight train. The ground almost liquid. In swimming pools, the water sloshed backwards and forwards, like when you get out of a bathtub. Things were crashing off the shelves.

Viola was on the big screen in the fallout shelter; scared. He yelled, "Are you okay?" The ground was still moving. She was yelling too. And looking at everything around her moving, falling, breaking.

Then it all stopped. But there was this sense that it would start again. Viola and Marlon waited for a few seconds.

Viola said, "I am okay. Please come up."

He said, "I want to." But he couldn't. He knew she was a predator. The tears were to fool him. The minute he came out, she would pounce.

He said, "I still have a lot to do. You should stop worrying. I'm going to pay the mortgage. It's on my to-do list. Things are looking up. Maybe I will buy you some diamond earrings. Maybe some shoes." And that car. He tells her all that. She starts pounding her hand on the kitchen counter for some reason. He must go. He has an important call coming in. He actually does. It's from me.

We connect on WhatsApp. He's *thought about it*, like he's some big player or something. He wants in. Of course he does. He's going to invest everything he has (and everything his family has), in the crypto coin, GRQ. Wise man. Glad I could help.

At that exact moment, he has two things on the computer screens in front of him. I know he does. The live chart with the GRQ price. It's steady. It's not made its move yet. The other screen is his bank balance. He is watching the payments from his family come into his account as he is talking to me. Nothing from his father-in-law yet. Of course. That means Marlon doesn't have enough to pay me the fifty thousand we agreed. So, he is going to try to buy time. From me. He must be joking.

He asks me for another explanation of crypto. I know what he is doing, and I almost say something, but I don't. People don't want to know they are one sandwich short of a full picnic. I am measuring the cost of my time against the potential profit here. I decide to give him a little time. I will talk about crypto, the currency of the future, before I bring down the hammer.

53. DE-FI

I can explain crypto without listening to myself. That's best. Not listening to yourself. So, you don't get involved in the necessary tawdry transactions of your own tawdry life. Just recite the litany. But don't listen. You'll get depressed.

I explain it: *Marlon, there's a revolution happening in the world of finance that is about money by the people and for the people. It's not about big bankers ripping you off, but ordinary people like you, sharing. This is cryptocurrency. The kumbaya of finance. The Buddhism of money makers. The sexually fluid, non-denominational anarcho-capitalism called De-fi. Decentralized finance. With no gatekeepers, rule makers, permission granters. Just you. A few million algorithm users, some blockchains and everyone is making money, and don't you want to?*

This is a sales technique. I don't know the meaning of a lot of the terms I am using here, like *non-denominational anarcho-capitalism*. I don't have a clue what that means. That's okay. People are drawn to what they half understand. They can fill in the other half with whatever they desire. Most people aren't seduced by things that are certain and have certain outcomes. Certainty is the end of hope. But the mysterious, not scientific and metaphysical? They can turn out any number of ways. Which means there can be hope, and the delusion of hope sustains us. This is my space. This is what I sell. Your lottery ticket might come up, despite the odds. If probability is wrong and science is wrong, then our expectations of potential outcomes can be limitless, and life is tolerable. I make life tolerable for my clients. So, they don't have to think about the empty space inside.

The easiest thing to sell in the world is a thing that is not understood. If it fails, it fails for secret purpose. If it succeeds, then mysterious forces are at work beyond our comprehension.

We want the world to be magical, and things that function without ostensible mechanisms, seem magical. Now you want to get into crypto sales, don't you?

I continued my lecture to Marlon: *Marlon, don't make it complicated. All you have to do is buy at one price and when it goes up, sell it. When it dips, you buy again. As for all your questions. Stop. You are asking what are cryptocurrency coins? How are they mined? How are they valued? Are you crazy? Think of it this way. You don't understand it. You won't understand it. But you will make money, and you won't know why. But if you make money, does it matter?*

Why do certain coins go up in value? The underlying reason? I have no fucking idea. But the other answer is because they become popular, because people think they will go up. It's like celebrities. Not the ones that can act, but the ones that can't. Suddenly, they become famous. Maybe they are in a TV show. It doesn't matter. They have acquired value because they have been identified as valuable. The fact they are popular makes them more popular. Don't overthink it. Your head will explode.

And Marlon, that's what your crypto investment is about. If you have a holding in a coin and it becomes popular, you get rich. How cool is that? Get Rich Quick. Ride the fucking wave.

And now comes GRQ. Those letters which will change your life, Marlon, because GRQ is special. These film producers I know are making a film about the GRQ coin. Will it be a good film? It doesn't matter. A bad film? It doesn't matter. A film that changes the world? It doesn't matter. When they announce the film about GRQ, everyone will presume that someone else will want to buy it because of the announcement. So, everyone will want to buy, because they think everyone else will buy because they think that everyone else will buy.

And Marlon, they are announcing it today at one o'clock, in only twenty minutes. So, it's the moment of truth for you, my friend. Time for you to pull the trigger. Unless you are too stupid to see sense.

It's good to insult people you are selling to, by calling them stupid for example. If you are nice, they think *you are selling*, but if you insult them, they know you are telling the truth. People are strange. Maybe they don't think very highly of themselves.

I make my play. I am going to close him. So I say:

Now is you in, or is you out?

Marlon is just smiling and looking at me, and I am thinking maybe he's medicated. Or he has lost the thread, or he is still overwhelmed with grief, that old canard. He keeps smiling. So, I keep smiling to keep the connection, even if he has lost the thread. Then I see the terror in his eyes. The absolute terror. Of saying or doing something that has a consequence. That can't be undone. I don't want to know his backstory. I don't want to think about his son. I don't want to look into his eyes. I want his money.

Marlon says, "Okay."

And I say, "Okay what?"

The clock says twelve forty-five. I say, "Marlon, *this is it, time for you to put in.*" Nothing. In my line of work, you dread this moment: he hesitates. What we call the second hesitation. This is the worst hesitation. Very often you never get them back after the second hesitation. You need to close people at the first pass, when they are freshly seduced; they are looking for confirmation. This is called the confirmation window. I may have dropped the ball. I may have missed the confirmation window.

I say: "Good choice, Marlon, you are a savvy investor." Another of my techniques. Suggesting he has led me to believe he has made a decision. Now he doesn't want to hurt my feelings. His finger is over the key on the computer that will send the wire with his money. I see his eyes. The terror is still there. The finger is still over the key.

54. BASED ON REAL EVENTS

Then things get strange. I go all out of body. I think I am in that crypto film those guys are making. I am not a film biz guy. I will get into it later with the money I make in crypto.

Imagine the movie: it starts with me on the screen. Next, there is Marlon, played by somebody famous. I will be open to ideas. Probably with a prosthetic something. So, the famous actor can really get into the character. Maybe big ears.

We see 'Marlon' thinking about the investment, deciding against it, deciding for it, deciding against it again and thinking his whole life and future are riding on this one decision.

Those film people screenwriters call this *increasing the stakes*. It's a trick they use to get us to care. They have professional tricks, just like I do. I guess we are all in show business, in one form or another. They also use something called *backstory*. You never want to hear a person's backstory in real life in business. But you do in a film. So, you care.

The audience is on the edge of their seats at this part. Will 'Marlon' invest, or won't he? He's taken money from everyone. They will all lose everything. That's a pretty horrible thought, now we know their back stories. Maybe some dramatic music? I notice film people use music at dramatic moments.

The audience wants to know *why doesn't he decide?* Exactly. He should; he is just delaying the inevitable. I get why the film people would stretch this moment out in their film. Because it's the moment before the big moment. That's where the tension lives.

I have seen a lot of movies. My aunt would take me to see French art films, in French. Without subtitles. We did that until they banned smoking in the theater. I am pretty sure she was the reason for the ban. Anyway, she told me, *it's the bit before the big moment that matters. Not the bomb going off, but the ticking of the timer on the bomb.*

In the movie, the famous actor playing 'Marlon' will be looking at 'me' on his big screen, looking at his 'wife' on the security camera, looking at pictures of his 'daughter' on his desk. Then, a really big moment. 'Marlon' looks up at one particular TV monitor in his fallout shelter/office/man cave and it is connected to security camera five pointed at an ***empty room that is dark and scary.*** And we don't know what it is. But the camera pushes into the scary image and then pushes into 'Marlon's' face and then *intense music (I am really sold on the music now)* and we realize this is a big moment, but the filmmaker hasn't explained it. So, they leave us to figure it out. Clever. Kind of a European or French filmmaking style. And we do. Figure it out. That's his dead son's room. *Christ.*

Later in the scene, the famous actor who is playing 'Marlon' is looking at his bank account, then he is looking at the sales video about GRQ, then he is looking at the GRQ price shooting upwards.

The filmmakers will also have a shot of the gun in the drawer. To add tension. The audience will think, why the sudden cut to the gun in the drawer? What does it mean? Oh my god, what will Marlon do if the price goes down? Or is it symbolic of something? Audiences will love it. It will become a world-famous movie. Un Film de...

Then the sequence will end, and then maybe 'Marlon' and 'Viola' (played by a famous actress) are kissing, or there is a car chase. I don't know.

As for the real-life Marlon, his finger is hovering over the keyboard. He still has that smile on his face. The clock is now only a few minutes before one. This is it. Now or never. The die is cast. The jib is up, the elevator is stopping at his floor.

Marlon has to learn that you must take risks or you're not alive. The plaque will build up in your veins and you mustn't dwell on the past. They're dead now and they can't hear your apologies, even if you call their cell phones. He pushes the key.

He is all in.

55. A BIG EVENT

Marlon's bank account balance falls to zero. Marlon feels sick. But GRQ is inching up.

For me, that ship had sailed, and I don't even remember if I said goodbye to him. I was onto the next client; the next one time only offer. I work hard. Selling, convincing, inspiring. Making people dare to dream doesn't sound hard, but if you don't think it's hard, you should try it. It's harder than unrequited love, or thimble collecting, or raising a child. Burying a child, that's harder. I admit it. But inspiring investors is also hard, okay?

Right after Marlon's big investment moment, he is phoning those people that wouldn't lend him money and telling them they made a *huge* mistake, and they should *stay tuned* for some *big news*. He tells them *it's top-secret*, and he can't tell them how or why, but he's about to come into some *serious money*.

He goes over to the whiteboard. He looks at the GRQ price. He calculates his earnings. Already 10K. He is on the road. *He can feel it*. He does a little dance. He is happy. He looks at the clock. It's coming up to one, and the big announcement.

Marlon turns on all the monitors to the financial channels. Steven Bernstein, the writer and director of GRQ appears on screen. Word must already be getting out because GRQ goes up some more. Bernstein is being interviewed and talking about his film GRQ and it's almost as if he is talking about Marlon's life. And mine.

They better not be. I know a lawyer from the gym. He gets big accident payments. We will sue Bernstein if Bernstein puts me in his movie without my permission.

If the lawsuit works out, maybe I can get involved in show business. I have several ideas for movies. I have seen a lot of French art films that could be remade.

Now Bernstein is talking more about the story of the film. Apparently, the film is about some guy getting in over his head on a crypto investment called GRQ. There is some shady sales guy. This is getting weird. They will be sorry.

Everyone does things for their own reasons. No self-important film guy should be judging anyone else. Then Bernstein starts wittering on about the morality of crypto, and whether it is okay to make profits from crypto. Seriously. Bernstein. Dude. Get a life.

I guess Bernstein must be doing this to make his film sound interesting. So, it makes more money. Oh wait, he just *slipped in* that there is a book as well. Of course. I am sure he is giving all the profits to some charity. Ha. Also, by talking about crypto he gets to sound morally superior to those of us who work for a living. Maybe I should make a film about him, see how he likes it.

Then it all goes wrong.

Bernstein and the host stop talking about the film's story and begin talking about how publicity drives crypto prices, rather than fundamentals and how dangerous it is for non-professional investors.

I am only half-watching. But Marlon is fully watching. He lets the fear in. Not good.

56. FEAR

1. Fear stops us from doing anything important.
2. Fear makes us live within our means, and smoke Gauloises.
3. Fear makes us hide things from our wives.
4. Fear makes us build fallout shelters.
5. Fear makes us not invest in things we don't understand.

Fear is like The Black Plague, Legionnaires' Disease, Smallpox, Influenza, Typhus, Cholera and Mad Cow Disease. It is deadly and it can infect a large population in a hurry.

Marlon's family is watching the show. And become frightened. Within minutes his father-in-law and his daughter and his mother are all phoning him. You could say, maybe he shouldn't have taken their money. Okay, maybe you have a point. But it was a once in a lifetime opportunity. Look, it had some possibilities. No question. But investment is a risk. Everyone should know that. You can't stop fear once it starts to spread. There is no vaccine for fear.

Marlon looks up at the security camera monitor and sees his wife on the phone to someone. She turns towards Marlon's camera and looks right down the barrel at him. He knows at that moment that she knows what he has done. That all their money is invested. And his mother's money. And his daughter's money, and her father's money. Some fucker has betrayed him. Another person hasn't believed in him. Another person has thrown him under the bus. He looks up again.

Viola is breaking things.

He wants to say, *Can we talk about this calmly?* But he knows that would make it worse. The smell of gas in the fallout shelter is making it worse. His past lies and failed businesses which were previously just elephants in the room, will now be marched in and paraded in a circle. He can't come up with a solution. This is what happens when people don't let him think. He needs to breathe. No one is letting him breathe. Or think. Everyone is phoning at once. It's not fair.

He doesn't pick up the phone, or Skype, or WhatsApp, or Google Hang-out. The calls are coming fast. They want to get to him, through every platform, every crack. Like that big crack in the ceiling he has never noticed before. It's really big now. Plaster is falling on his desk. He goes to the punching bag. Hits it. Again, faster and harder. His knuckle bleeds. Bernstein finally shuts up and smiles as the show ends. Not caring about the damage he has caused, the destruction, obviously a sociopath. Marlon walks around the room, trying hard to think.

He looks at the GRQ price and puts its graph up on all the screens so he can watch it more. It ticks...

1. Down.
2. Then down some more.
3. And more.
4. He opens the drawer with the gun.
5. He takes it out.
6. GRQ is still going down.
7. He begins aiming the gun at things around the room.
8. He looks at the photographs of his family on his desk and on the wall.
9. Him and his wife.
10. GRQ is still going down.
11. Him and his wife, his son, and his daughter.
12. Him and his son.
13. Then one just of his son.
14. Then another, just his son.
15. GRQ is still going down.
16. And GRQ is still going down.

He looks out of the corner of his eye at the monitor that is connected to security camera number five that is always pointing at the empty, dark room. He begins to squeeze the trigger and...

BANG!

The gun goes off.

The bullet makes a huge noise and ricochets around the hard walls of the room.

God knows where it will land. Marlon checks his body.

He is okay. He thinks, "That was exciting." And then, "I nearly shot myself."

57. NOT LOOKING

A few years before this, Marlon was in his fallout shelter/office/man cave and he was watching things on all his screens. Football, a news show, and a rerun of an old film. At the same time. It made him feel busy and kinda important.

What he wasn't looking at was the **black and white security camera number five**. The one down the hall from his son's room. Darien's room. He didn't see Darien crying in his room. Or the notes to his sister, and his mother and to him. His beautiful boy. Marlon might have glanced up at that moment. But he didn't. The football game was being decided by a field goal. The old film was at its powerful end and the music was soaring. The news show had something about housing values going down. There was so much drawing Marlon's attention, that he was distracted. Security camera number five pointed at Darien's half-open door. Marlon could have looked at security camera number five at any time. He just didn't. So he didn't see Darien attach the rope to the ceiling or put the rope around his neck and jump off the chair.

When someone hangs themselves, sometimes it breaks the spinal cord.

But sometimes it doesn't.

The rope applies a lot of pressure on the jaw, so the tongue protrudes out, causing it to dry. It also causes a narrowing up of the laryngeal and tracheal lumina and forcing up of the root of the tongue against the posterior wall of the pharynx and that blocks the airflow. The jugular vein is also blocked, due to the ligature increasing pressure inside the head, which causes death. Marlon looked up and saw his son's hanging feet through the half-open door and ran to his room, much too late.

The field goal was good by the way. The credits rolled on the old film, and the news show started a segment on all the rain California had been having recently.

58. OBJECTS OF THEIR ARDOR

So, Marlon had fired the gun. But there were eighteen-inch thick walls, so nobody heard. He stands up. One of those silences again. Just him and him, his eyes shut. He isn't paying attention. Again.

Behind him on the big screen, something is moving.

Moving on all the screens. But he doesn't see. It is GRQ. It has reversed course. He isn't looking. GRQ isn't just climbing. It is shooting up. 100, 120, 140, 150. Up.

He turns around. He sees. Quieter than before, but joy, he dances some more. He shouts. He screams. It isn't just happiness. It's a release. He pounds on the desk. He cries again. More than crying, a body-shaking, unrelenting sob. He can do that here, with the eighteen-inch thick walls around him. No one will know or see; he is by himself. He wants to say, *I am not such a loser now, am I?*

He does some calculations on the whiteboard. He just made 120k. Just like that, he's more than halfway there. It's still climbing.

He looks up at security camera number three, to see what his wife is doing. Her anger seems to have gone away. That's good. Soon they will be able to talk, *calmly*. But he sees she is moving with purpose. She is packing her bags. In the bedroom. This is bad.

Then he sees the thimble that the old woman had given her on the bedside table. Then he sees his wife is packing her jewelry. This is real. This is bad. Marlon doesn't know much about thimbles. People who collect them are called digitabulists. A Meissen porcelain thimble sold for 20,000 dollars. Thimbles were invented so people sewing wouldn't poke themselves with needles. There was a lot of sewing through many centuries, so a lot of thimbles. Thimbles were made of metal, wood, glass, china, leather, marble, semi-precious stones, mother of pearl, whalebone, horn and ivory. Queen Elizabeth the First gave one of her ladies-in-waiting a thimble, inlaid with precious jewels. Paul Revere made one of gold. Sometimes lovers would give them to the objects of their ardor.

I remember my aunt sitting under a tree and she was reading poetry to me, and I remember being happy, and even my aunt, who never seemed really happy, seemed a little happy. And she said the word *ardor,* and I asked her what it meant, and she said, "A feeling that is so intense, it is stronger than love or sense or even caring about yourself anymore. It makes you want, and it makes you not want to want because the wanting is so strong. It's something you care about so much and can't control it or hold it or keep it."

I am not sure this was the right definition. My aunt would get sort of lost sometimes, mixing up all sorts of things in her head: right, wrong, saving me, abandoning me, loving me and hurting me. But I still wonder why, when all the ardor is over, when a thing's history is all that is left, free of its emotional connections, why those digitabulists value those thimbles? Or why any of us value anything that doesn't have a function in our lives anymore? I wish, just once in my life, I could feel the ardor my aunt described. But I guess that ship has sailed.

59. CROSSING THE RUBICON

Marlon realizes the Rubicon has been crossed. He was never quite sure what a Rubicon was. But crossing it was bad. You always sense that you can live inside a certain space, like a relationship, and all sorts of things can happen there, but even in relationships, there is always a Rubicon. You just don't know it's there. It kinda hides. Waiting for you to really mess up.

Marlon runs to the heavy door and starts opening it. If they talk calmly, maybe they won't have to cross any Rubicons. Another call. His daughter and her husband Michael appear on a screen. He doesn't want to take this call but he has to. Because he took their money.

Michael is trembling with rage. It is overwhelming him. Possessing him. Marlon has crossed his Rubicon. You can have more than one Rubicon. If you aren't careful, you can be crossing Rubicons, left and right. Michael is livid that Marlon talked his own daughter into lending him money.

Investing, Marlon corrects him.

Fuck you, Michael corrects back.

Well, not corrected. But expressed strongly. Not understanding the situation at all. And doing his own Rubicon crossing, if you ask Marlon. Rubicons can cut both ways. Michael wants their money back.

What he says precisely is: "We want our money back, you fucking thief." Michael doesn't get the non-scientific words like *impressions* and *performance*, or the *changing nature* of things based on *popularity*. He wants things to be predictable and quantifiable. So, he would never understand, for example, show business. Or crypto currency. He is limited in many ways. But Sarah can't see it. She is too busy telling him she loves him to really consider his nature. Trying to make their relationship perfect. Probably not yet counting the days between arguments.

Sarah does ask Michael to *stop talking that way* to her father. He doesn't. He doesn't understand, Marlon needs to hold onto their money until they have made a lot of money. It would be bad business practice to take the money out before it has made big profits.

Then Sarah, his one surviving child, says, softly: "Daddy, please give it back. Please."

One of those silences again that Marlon hates. It is during the silences he thinks of things he cannot think about anymore. And then Michael begins to yell again, so Marlon has to hang up.

Marlon feels bad for his daughter. She has got herself into a bad situation. He looks up again at the big monitor. Viola has finished packing. She is taking the bags off the bed. Before she leaves, she will be phoning Darien again. Darien won't be picking up, of course. But she will still leave another long, rehearsed message. It must be nearly fully by now, his phone. Marlon thinks again he should cancel the line. But he is worried about Viola dialling it again and a recording telling her that the phone has ceased to exist. And her son has ceased to exist.

Another call comes in. He takes this one because it is his mother. She is beaming. She is so proud of him. He has made so much money. She was watching. Also, the drain is making a funny noise. Like a glugging sound. Also, the woman across the street watches her through her curtains. Could Marlon come over? Could he put the money he borrowed back in her bank?

"Investment," he says.

"And I love you, son. I am so proud of you." And she's gone.

Sarah is phoning again. He doesn't pick up. She leaves a message. He only listens to the beginning. *Please, Daddy...*Viola appears on the big screen. Like the Wizard of Oz. He answers, relieved. She hasn't left yet. Viola speaks:

"My father? Without telling me? And all your big stories. And now we are going to lose the house? Your endless lies. I can't take it anymore."

Another long silence.

And Marlon looks at security camera number five, looking into that dark room. Still. The same angle. The parts he couldn't see.

And Marlon says, "It wasn't my fault."

And Viola says, "It is your fault."

And Marlon says, "It wasn't my fault." Then she knows what he is talking about.

She pauses. Then she says, "Nobody said it was your fault. It wasn't anyone's fault."

He says, "But I am a loser. Aren't I?"

And Viola says, "It doesn't matter anymore."

And Marlon says, "Do you blame me?"

And Viola says, "I miss him."

And Marlon says, "I tried. I try."

And Viola says, "Now all this, Marlon. I can't forgive you anymore. And our house? What will happen to us?"

And Marlon hangs his head and says, "It's going up. Really." He tries to turn the camera on the computer screen to show her, but he can't figure out how to point one screen at the other for some reason. Too much multi-tasking. And too many cables.

It's all a tangle of wires and screens.

And as he tries to maneuver the screens, GRQ begins to plunge down again. At speed. Down, down, down.

Marlon hangs up on his wife and phones me. Me! No way am I picking up. Anyway, GRQ going down is a good thing. Dips are a good thing, because it gives you an opportunity to buy some more. To average. Marlon should have been buying the dips. Except, of course, he doesn't have any money. And now he is losing other people's money. What they all had to understand was the right philosophy in these circumstances is HODL. Hold on for dear life. With white knuckles. Which is a good general principle in life. Because, really, anyway, what choice do we have?

His family is hysterical, and emotional, and you shouldn't be trading when you are emotional. Marlon keeps phoning me. I did him a favor by giving him this opportunity.

I can understand, scientifically, why everyone is so upset. The GRQ price is going down. Like in those Road Runner cartoons, when Wile E. Coyote goes off a cliff ledge, and there is that whistling sound, and then he drops to the bottom of the canyon and there is a little thud.

I had already sold my personal holding in GRQ just two points off its high.

You could accuse me of 'pump-and-dump'. If by that you mean I got people to buy GRQ to push the price up and then I sold my own holding at a profit, leaving them stuck, well, then, you would be right.

But I am allowed to do what I want with my own money. Right? As for the others, well, I couldn't force them to sell, and they didn't ask me if they should, until GRQ was dropping like Wile E. Coyote. It's not like the stock market. It's not regulated. I don't just take orders like a waiter. If they wanted that sort of service, they should have gone to one of the full-service trading companies. Lots of people do. But I charge a lot less.

And I am a lot more fun.

And willing to give brave, radical, imaginative advice.

And you don't even have to say thank you.

60. THE END OF THE WORLD

It is four twenty in the afternoon. Only forty minutes left for Marlon to save his home. Marlon is sitting in the middle of that fallout shelter, and he has taken the gun out and put it on his desk. All the phones and the computer and anything that will buzz, or beep or vibrate is doing just that, and Marlon is watching the price going down. Like Wile E. Coyote. The crack in the ceiling is huge now. The gas smell is worse, and the air conditioner has stopped working. The televisions are all so loud. Then, worse than before, everything begins to shake violently. This is it. The big one. A massive earthquake.

All those earthquakes that went before had been building to this. The noise seems to come from the center of the earth, a colossal earthquake. The ground deep beneath Marlon's feet liquefies.

Buildings begin to collapse all over LA.

Part of the 101 freeway collapses. The high-rises in downtown Los Angeles are swaying wildly.

Marlon's house is shaking and swaying, bouncing, breaking and finally falling apart. The house is just above the epicenter.

Everything is falling in his fallout shelter. The lights are flickering, and all the hundreds of canned goods fall over and roll around on the floor. The air at the top of the room suddenly ignites and burns wildly. The leaked gas. Marlon, in his confusion, can only think it looks like a special effect in a film; it's so odd to see the air burning. Then magically, it stops, but there seems to be little air left in the room. It is hard for Marlon to breathe.

Marlon is looking at all the security cameras, and he sees things falling all over his house. Outside, he sees cars bouncing like toys and a water main break and a plume of water shoot forty feet into the air. Inside, he sees Viola in the kitchen, screaming, as all the dishes fall, and everything is breaking and a moment later the roof caves in on top of her and the screen is blocked by dust and plaster.

Marlon goes running for the door, when the wall of the fallout shelter buckles also, and then the roof of the fallout shelter caves in. Then all the lights and all the monitors shut off. The shaking continues for a while and then stops. Marlon is in blackness. Silence. He is in a sort of tomb. Minutes pass. Then the emergency generator kicks in. After all those years, waiting for the nuclear Armageddon, it finally got its opportunity. Then all the screens come back on. There are news stories on every screen about the quake.

Marlon digs himself out from the rubble. He phones Viola. *We are sorry for the interruption of service in your area.*

Marlon calls his daughter. She and Michael answer. Some things have fallen over, but they are okay. Marlon sees his baby grandson in his daughter's arms. He's named after her brother, Darien. They ask about Viola. He doesn't know; he's trying to see through the dust of the kitchen. He's frantic. Michael is going to come over, but it will take a while; the freeways are blocked.

A Skype call. His mother. She is covered in dust. Holding her cat, Rupert, also covered in dust. But she is okay. She is worried about them. She is thinking of Darien. How much they all miss him. She tells Marlon she loves him, and she is proud of him, whether he made a lot of money in crypto or not. He asks if her house is okay. She says it's only things.

He tries Viola again. *We are sorry for the interruption of service in your area.*

Another call appears on a screen. His father-in-law, Charles, and next to him, Judy, still with her private smile, still lost.

Charles asks him how he is and about Viola. Marlon explains as best he can. There is a moment of them connecting. Like they are both adults, sorting out a problem. Charles nods at him, Marlon, covered in dust, like a soldier in a trench. And Marlon, feeling like an adult, nods back. And Charles says, "You do what you must do there son. We will check in a little later, Judy and I."

Marlon looks at GRQ. It's still going down. Does it even matter anymore?

Marlon begins pushing against the heavy door. It is jammed.

He looks at the devastation in the kitchen and at the other cameras in the rest of the house. There isn't much intact. Is she dead? He pushes the door some more. It moves a few inches. But it doesn't open. He keeps pushing. He jams a bit of board in with some success. As he makes progress, he jams in some vintage cans of Spam. He looks behind him. On three screens, Sarah, his mother, and Charles and Judy are all watching. He sees the devastation of LA on another screen. He sees the GRQ chart on another screen…and then, he sees on the intercom camera that is just outside the fallout shelter, his wife by the fallout shelter door. Pulling at it from the outside. She is alive.

Now he leans on the wood beam, pushing, as she pulls, as if all the things they couldn't control in the past, are now seemingly embodied in that heavy door. All their pain, all their dreams, all their confusion at the disorder of the world. My aunt once said, *In chaos there is hope, if not resurrection*. She also said, *There is no un-ringing of any bell*. They are working. So hard. If only effort could alter the unalterable. If only effort and need, determined outcome. Finally, the door moves.

Viola stumbles in, and they embrace.

And that's when I call in, and Marlon, for reasons I cannot fathom, answers. I am surprised to see them both, of course. And all the mayhem. I have my own problems, but still, I look in. He is a client, after all. I am thinking of the long term.

They barely look at me, so anxious to say to each other how much they love one another, and how Marlon will tell her no more lies, how he will show his weakness and his pain, how they will build a life together for themselves, even if they have nothing left. And I think they believe all of that. Because hope is what I sell, and I know the language of selling when I hear it, and if you pitch hope just right, people will believe you, because they believe in it themselves even without a pitch.

I figure, it would be a good time to see if they want to cut their losses. They are just about to answer, when they notice that GRQ is going straight up, like a rocket. Something to do with the earthquake, if you want to attribute causality to crypto prices. That would be misguided. But don't let me stop you. Marlon and Viola turn and look at the screen. So, I ask them again, "Should I sell?" and they look at each other, and then look again at the GRQ chart, and it is still going up.

EPILOGUE

It seemed as if the earth would swallow Los Angeles on that day. But in a few weeks, they were rebuilding houses and bridges and fixing roads, and people moved to where they were before. Pretty much. They know more quakes will come but are sure they'll be okay. However, they think others should be worried, what with all the quakes in the area. There was a little one in Malibu and a house slipped off the hill. The big brush fire was much worse.

The guy at Frank's on La Brea where I bought the lottery tickets, was found dead behind his counter one afternoon. Several customers (and probably some cranks) came in and stole spirits and beer while he was lying there on the floor. It was three hours before anyone reported it to the police.

The guy at the desk at The Polo Lounge, who gave Marlon the funny looks, borrowed some money from friends and relatives and opened a contemporary Indian/American fusion restaurant in North Hollywood. But it was a bad location, and he was forced to close in eighteen months. He couldn't get his old job back at The Polo Lounge so ended up as a waiter in a Mediterranean restaurant in a strip mall on Pico.

The valet at The Beverly Hills Hotel kept doing his acting classes in The Valley and got cast in a long-running cop procedural show as an eccentric homeless person, who is secretly working for the police. He did it for three years and then moved back to Minnesota.

The receptionist at the mortgage company became a mortgage broker.

The Jewish cemetery where Mr. Liebowitz was buried had several stones fall over in the earthquake, and later it was vandalized by some neo-Nazis who painted a swastika on Mr. Liebowitz's tombstone, which a volunteer group eventually cleaned off. But then more neo-Nazis painted another swastika, and I am not sure if that one has been removed.

The cab driver sold an option on his screenplay for a few hundred dollars, with the understanding that he would get a hundred and fifty thousand dollars when and if the film based on the screenplay got made. He let the producers renew the option twice for very small sums, but they never raised the money. He stopped driving and would always thereafter introduce himself as a writer with a project in development with a Hollywood production company.

Steven Bernstein, the film director, gave up his day job.

My aunt's house was sold to a couple who gutted the interior and repainted the exterior, so that when I drove by it once years later, I barely recognized the place. It sold for a lot more money than my aunt could have ever imagined. And even with the money we might have made from the investments, from the cash I took from the pawnbrokers, we probably couldn't have bought it back, even if she wanted to. Anyway, I think she would rather have been in France. As for the guy in France, she never heard from him. Neither did I, though I tried writing to various addresses that I found on those letters that she never sent. I did get one mysterious envelope, with a photograph of an old, unattractive man inside and I thought, surely, he couldn't be the one that all the fuss was about. I mean thirty years of her life; he should have looked like Cary Grant. There wasn't even a note inside. Maybe desire isn't always proportional to the quality of the thing desired.

As for Viola and Marlon, well, that's a secret I must keep. Although I heard that Marlon changed his focus to AI recently.

As for their son, he was never resurrected. Though his memory was, at regular intervals. And he, like the elephant, was always in their room for the rest of their natural lives.

And as for me? You will remember I am the maker of dreams. A merchant of hope. But in the end, as nothing I stole or earned, or gained or loved had any substantive value, there was nothing for me to covet or hold and no reason for me to remain.

ACKNOWLEDGMENTS

There is a book to be written about the writing of this book. It will also be much longer than this book, though perhaps not as good. Still, the tangling together of what is on these pages, my life, a film, and various misadventures may be edifying, given the eventual luxury of time. But that's *that* book. This book is something else.

My wife, Carolyn Rodney, read every word of each iteration. I can't say her incisive remarks were always kind, but they were appropriate, smart, and made the book better. So that is the greatest kindness. Also, without her encouragement, there would be no book, no film, and not much else either. I am grateful.

My son knows me better than he should; I would prefer to have a mythological standing of some sort, though it wouldn't have been deserved. Remarkably, he took a great deal of time to read what I wrote and make observations and suggestions that altered both my thinking and my writing. His is a particularly brilliant mind and a gently, patient temperament.

Clare Coombs is my literary agent at The Liverpool Literary Agency. She spent and still spends an absurd amount of time getting this book out to the world, looking after my interests, guiding me, and quietly educating me about the literary world, publishing, and the capriciousness of human nature. She is wise and generous. Again, without her, there would be no book.

Isabelle Kenyon leads Fly on the Wall Press, who have published GRQ, and her vision, hard work, intelligence, and perseverance make it impossible for me to understand how anyone can get a book out who doesn't have an Isabelle to lead them over the rampart. A radical thinker and a practical mind. I am grateful.

My friend Muwaffaq Salti read an early version of this book, and it became a conversation that carried on for over a year. His sharp mind profoundly influenced every page of this book.

The absurdly industrious Jonathon Nimmons put the publishing of this book in motion by believing in the book and in me and connecting me to the gifted and generous John Maxwell, which led me to Clare. We like to think we find our way through our force of will. As it turns out, it is the kindness of others.

The book is now also a feature film called GRQ. There is a too-long list of people to thank for that film, so I will here just thank everyone involved in that project en masse. It is a wonderful thing.

ABOUT THE AUTHOR

Steven Bernstein ASC, DGA, WGA is a screenwriter and director based in Los Angeles and the UK. He was born in Buffalo in upstate New York and lived in the United Kingdom for twenty-eight years, before moving to Los Angeles. He still balances his life and work between the two countries.

His new feature film, GRQ, is based on his novella starring Mena Suvari. He directed from his script. It is released later this year. Before that, he wrote and directed the award-winning LAST CALL, which stars John Malkovich and Rhys Ifans.

Previously, he directed the award-winning Decoding Annie Parker, also from his script, which starred Samantha Morton and Helen Hunt. He has written over forty screenplays.

He has a new book coming out next year called The Creative Process to be published by Routledge, who also published his earlier book. He writes for several magazines and his podcast, Filmmaker and Fan has several million listeners.

Before he was a screenwriter and director he was a cinematographer, shooting the Oscar winning Monster among some sixty-three other films and television shows, including some of the highest grossing studio features of their type. He was an American Society of Cinematographers nominee for his work on Magic City and has won many other awards. He has worked in motion pictures and television for over forty years.

He has traveled and lectured widely and shot films and commercials in some twenty-six countries. He is a member of the Director's Guild of America, The American Society of Cinematographers and the Writer's Guild of America.

About Fly on the Wall Press

A publisher with a conscience.
Political, Sustainable, Ethical.
Publishing politically-engaged, international fiction, poetry and cross-genre anthologies on pressing issues. Founded in 2018 by founding editor, Isabelle Kenyon.

Some other publications:

The Soul We Share by Ricky Ray

The Unpicking by Donna Moore

Lying Perfectly Still by Laura Fish

Modern Gothic - Anthology Edited by Isabelle Kenyon

And I Will Make of You a Vowel Sound by Morag Anderson

The Dark Within Them by Isabelle Kenyon

The Wager and the Bear by John Ironmonger

The Process of Poetry Edited by Rosanna McGlone

The Others by Sheena Kalayil

Demos Rising - Anthology Edited by Isabelle Kenyon

Your Sons and Your Daughters Are Beyond by Rosie Garland

The Truth Has Arms and Legs by Alice Fowler

The Devil's Draper by Donna Moore

The State of Us by Charlie Hill

The Sleepless by Liam Bell

Social Media:

@fly_press (X)

@flyonthewallpress (Instagram, Bluesky, Facebook, Tiktok)

www.flyonthewallpress.co.uk